BEAUTY'S KISS

PART III OF THE *ONCE UPON A PRINCESS* SAGA

C. S. Johnson

Library of Congress Control Number: 2017909187

ISBN-13 eBook: 9781943934-287

ISBN-10 eBook: 1-943934-28-2

ISBN-13 Book: 9781943934-294

ISBN-10 Book: 1-943934-29-0

For Sam. The heart has its reasons, whereas reason has lost its mind.

This is also for my own darling prince and princess—may you never once believe you are alone in this world, so long as you know the truth and the truth of my love for you.

C. S. JOHNSON

This book is published courtesy of

www.direwolfbooks.com

PART III

"Everything in the world has a hidden meaning.
Men, animals, trees, stars, they are all hieroglyphics.
When you see them you do not understand them.
You think they are really men, animals, trees, stars.
It is only years later that you understand."
~ Nikos Kazantzakis

1

ONCE UPON A PRINCESS

2

1

The small, persistent beam of sunlight crept through the narrow crevices of the distant mountains, its determined line breaking out from behind the clouds, cutting through the pockets of night and the early morning fog. Rose was transfixed by the sight before her, enraptured by the staggering amount of simple delight it gave her. The edge of Crystal Lake, for which the kingdom of Philip's sister-in-law was named, was in sight at last.

Now, Rose thought, *all I have to do is get back to Rhone, and Magdalina's reign will end.*

Rose glanced down at the ruby shining in the hilt of her sword. The slim beam of sunlight teased out its darkened red heart, where the dragon's blood resided.

A small burst of pride soared inside of her; Rose knew what the deadly jewel had cost her, but it was well worth the price she'd paid. Since leaving Poiyana, the city in the heart of the Romani territory, she had the power she knew she would need to destroy her greatest foe.

Rose continued to stare at the scene before her, as she folded her arms and leaned back against the sturdy tree behind her. *Good. We're here. That means we can finally say goodbye to Natala.*

Rose wasn't sure if she was happy to see the Crystal Lake Kingdom more for its beauty, or because it meant she would be free of Natala; the middle-aged woman traveled across the continent for her living, but it seemed more like she drew her sustenance from sucking the life out of her clients' souls.

Not even the prickly bark grabbing the growing hair at her shoulders could dampen Rose's spirits at the thought of leaving Natala behind.

As he had promised, Nikolai, their guide through the Romani mountains, had introduced them to his sister, Natala. He had told them she was more than willing to lead them back through the worlds between the Romani territory and the small kingdom of Crystal Lake.

Much to Rose's dismay, it turned out Natala's temperament was far from the gruff, philosophizing manner of her brother's. Rose was certain she'd never known a woman more capable at setting her temper ablaze with her constant criticizing and perpetual moaning.

Rose sighed and bowed her head, squirming only a little as her hair pulled free from the bark. On some level, she had to wonder if she deserved the small twinge of pain. She knew it was a very practical thing, to have a skilled guide along for the ride. It was also a very fortunate thing, since they were navigating across the Romani plains, traveling through the northern passages of Greek territories, walking through the Apylian Mountains, and drifting down the Gaullian riverways. Natala had promised, for half the price upfront, to take them to Crystal Lake, where Prince Derick, Philp's older brother, would be holding court.

She knew she should be grateful.

But if she had to do it all over again, Rose would any other way to go; she would even choose to go by boat, a shocking revelation in itself, since they had been shipwrecked on an island and blown off course for days in their latest attempts to cross the great seas. Rose never thought she would be content to set sail again.

She felt better knowing that she was not the only one who had trouble with the bad-tempered guide. Over the past several weeks, she had a wide range of small talks with her traveling companions, whether to talk them down from their irritation or to have them chastise her for her own disgust.

Even Theo has had a hard time dealing with Natala.

Rose felt surprised, as she smiled her first fully genuine smile in weeks. The thought of her best friend struggling to hold back his temper was amusing in the worst sort of way.

"You seem happy this morning. I hope you're not thinking of drowning Natala in the lake," Theo said. He appeared beside her suddenly, and Rose nearly jumped at his voice; she wondered if she had been that distracted by the scenery not to notice his approach.

"I wasn't," she promised.

"That's good to hear. It would have been unpleasant to fight you for the privilege."

Rose laughed before she quickly covered her mouth with her hand. She knew she had to be careful not to wake anyone, especially Natala.

"I wouldn't worry about waking her," Theo said, as if he had known what she was thinking. "Philip managed to get her some more wine last night, and she'll sleep longer thanks to that."

"Well, thank God for Philip," Rose whispered back, still trying to stifle her giggles. "We should have figured out her weakness weeks ago."

"I'm in complete agreement," Theo said, "even if I would have to repent for it later."

"I don't think God should hold it against you." Rose rolled her eyes. "Surely he would not be adverse to us putting her to sleep, especially if it means we don't actually kill her."

"There is no sin greater than another."

"Come on, Theo, let me rationalize any possible guilt away."

He smiled at her. "If we could only rationalize away the things we feel all the time."

Despite the simple, seemingly harmless reply, Rose felt the heat rise in her cheeks as she experienced a mix of guilt and mortification. There were some feelings she did wish that she could rationalize away, banishing them at the mere thought. She had spent a good portion of the trip trying to do just that, but there were plenty of reasons to keep that from Theo.

She glanced over at him now, seeing the warmth in his emerald eyes, and she decided it was best to change the subject. "I guess we are getting closer to Rhone. You should probably be practicing all that priestly stuff again, if you are going to visit with your grandfather and Thad at the church in Havilah."

"I might have been raised in the church, but I would have thought all this time traveling would have shown you I don't intend to stay there."

His words were measured and calm, but Rose could have sworn there was a bite underneath them. She could not resist replying spitefully. "Well, all this time we've been traveling should have done a better job of drumming it out of you."

He shrugged as she huffed. He turned back to face the lake water, allowing her a moment to stare at him openly without fear or hesitation.

Certain he was not able to see her expression, Rose allowed herself to blush without restraint. Over the past month since they had left Poiyana, Rose had been unable to forget that moment in the inn.

Theo had been sitting across from her, his shirt was off since Mary had just finished applying a new layer of healing ointment to the wounds he had sustained in their fight against the Thorneback dragon. And while she was confessing the worst of who she was, he had only placed his hands around her face, and drawn her close to him. Rose was convinced if they hadn't been interrupted, he would have kissed her.

And she would have let him.

Nothing about that moment had left her memory. She could close her eyes and slip into it all over again. Sometimes her dreams let her do more than remember it.

Rose felt that tension inside of her return in vengeful force as she peeked over at him, as he stood next to her, looking out into the distance at Crystal Lake.

Neither of them had said anything about it.

But Rose knew she was thinking about it. And she had a feeling he was, too. For all their trouble with Natala and dealing with the harsh elements of traveling on the road, there were times when she would look up to see him watching her, or she would catch herself staring at him, and something would rise inside of her, and she would have to force it down again.

She cleared her throat, trying to rid herself of any remaining wonderings. Rose had closed the door on romance and true love a long time ago, and she was not about to let anyone change her mind—not even Theo.

"So," she said, "how long do you think it will be until everyone else is up and ready to go?"

"If you can convince them there will be a comfortable bed and a warm dinner, I'm sure it won't take long."

"I'll make that Philip's first job this morning then," Rose decided. "He should have a better idea of what kind of hospitality we should expect here."

"From everything he's told me so far, we should be quite welcome."

"He would be; it remains to be seen about the rest of us."

"Crystal Lake has a good reputation for taking in strangers," Theo said. He reached over and pulled a lock of her hair free from the clinging crevices of the tree bark behind her. "And I have yet to see someone who wasn't charmed by you."

Rose stiffened, paralyzed with fear and, to her self-horror, longing as well. Forcing herself to breathe normally, she stepped forward. She gripped her sword with renewed determination. "I guess I can always evoke Isra's name," she said, thinking of her younger sister. "Since she's pretending to be engaged to Philip."

"I forgot about that. That would work, too. If the news has reached to this part of the kingdom, that is."

He was so infuriating, Rose thought. Theo was acting so … so normal! She was standing only a foot away from him, suffering even while she enjoyed his company, as she had done an uncountable number of times before. Why was it different now?

Or, she admitted very, very softly to herself, was it just harder for her to ignore how much she wanted him, now that she had admitted it?

That moment of surrender, of submission, sank into her once more, and inside she reeled at its force.

She needed to find another distraction, she thought. "How are your injuries?" Rose asked.

"They seem to be getting better. Mary said the scars will still be visible across my back, but that doesn't bother me." He ran a hand through his black hair, pushing it back from his face. "I remember my dad and my uncle had plenty of battle scars."

"I guess it is a sign of accomplishment," Rose said. She almost reached out for him, knowing it was hard for him to talk about his family even after so many years had passed. But this time, her pervasive and unpredictable thoughts kept her from offering him comfort.

"Not everyone can boast of an encounter with a dragon," Theo said.

Rose nodded. "That alone should make it easy to promote you to the royal counsel."

His eyes gleamed appreciatively. "When you are Queen of Rhone, I will remind you of that."

You won't have to remind me, Rose felt like telling him. But she only nodded again.

Weighed silence passed between them again, as they looked at each other. Theo took a step closer to her. "Rose—"

They were swiftly interrupted as Natala's voice screeched out in angry tones, crying out from their camp. "Oh, my head!"

Rose and Theo both looked back.

"Where's my wine?" she cried. "Why didn't someone get me up sooner? Why aren't the rest of you up? We're almost there. Get up. Get up!"

"Great," Rose muttered. "She's awake."

"And she's moving," Theo said, cringing as various clanks and clashes rang out in the background as Natala began scrounging around, dumping out supplies and tripping over the others.

"Let's just hope she doesn't get into Sophie's tools again," Rose muttered. "Sophie was not happy about all the iron filings in Natala's hands, and Mary wasn't able to help her remove them any."

"I'm more worried she'll step on Ethan's harp again. When she stepped on it last week, I was pretty sure Ethan was going to cry."

"On the upside, he has been doing better at his training, since his harp needs repairs," Rose said. "I've noticed you've been teaching him more advanced techniques lately."

"I'd still hate for his motivation to be compromised—or inspired—by Natala," Theo replied. "We'd better get over there before everyone's in a bad mood."

"I guess I better get Philip up." Rose pursed her lips. "Natala is making this unpleasant."

Theo laughed. "We'll make it through, Rosary," he promised. "I said my prayers this morning."

ONCE UPON A PRINCESS

2

"And this is where you'll be sleeping," Philip said, as he gallantly pushed open the door to an unoccupied bedroom. "As you can see, it'll be much more comfortable than camping on the ground."

"Humph! I wouldn't have come up this far if I didn't think it was worth it," Natala grumbled. Her long hair, tucked back into a bun mixed with gray and brown, pulled free as she pushed past the others to enter her room.

Theo watched with sympathy as Philip's polite smile tightened with underlying irritation. The Prince of Einish was among the most even-tempered men he knew, but after weeks of Natala's complaints, even he was clearly glad she would be leaving soon.

Of course, not soon enough for Philip, by the looks of it, Theo thought. But it was safe to say that was probably true for the rest of their company, too.

"Well," Philip said, "please feel free to ring for anything that you need."

"I can just tell you what I need now," Natala said. "I'll need some extra blankets, and I'll need some laundry done, and something finer to wear while my laundry is getting done, and then I'll need some spirits to drink so my poor knees and back will have some relief, and then … "

"Just close the door on her," Rose ordered in a fierce whisper. "She's not looking. We can say you didn't hear her."

Philip, without hesitation, shut the door behind him. "I'll be happy to tell her that I heard her, I just didn't listen. I am a prince, after all. That stuff doesn't fall to me. But I will be

11

making sure that whoever it does fall to will be amply reward-
ed."

"Does Crystal Lake have any prisoners who might be up
for the job?" Ethan scoffed.

"They have a rule about cruel and unusual punishment
here," Philip said.

"Too bad." Ethan frowned. "After what she did to my
harp, she deserves to be punished."

"I think Philip was saying that serving her would be too
cruel a punishment, little brother," Sophia said, as she came
up and laid a comforting hand on his shoulder. "But either
way, I'm sure someone will take care of her."

"We do have several craftsmen on staff, Ethan," Philip
said. "Derick is always hunting, so he makes sure he has plenty of repairmen around, too. I'll be happy to take your harp
down to the shops and see about getting it fixed up properly."

"I'd rather do it myself." Ethan scrunched up his face. "It'll
give me something to do other than think about hitting her."

Rose cleared her throat, trying not to laugh. She knew
Ethan still missed his harp instructor, Penelope. He worked
hard to make sure that he kept up with his music, even
though it had been some time since he had heard from her.
While Ethan was able to send her a few letters over the last
month, he knew it would be a long time before he was able to
see her again. Rose did not want to see his innocent dreams
of true love to be lost, and she did not want someone like
Natala to cause him to lose hope.

"Alright, everyone," Rose said. "Let's not worry about
Natala anymore. She is an older lady, and there's plenty in her
life I'm sure none of us have ever had to deal with. She'll be

gone from Crystal Lake before too long, and in the meantime, we need not bother with her ourselves."

"Thank the good Lord," Sophia muttered.

Rose turned her attention to Philip. "Alright, *that's* taken care of," she said. "Now, show the rest of us where we'll be sleeping. Mary's still tired. I'm sure a proper mattress will make her sublimely happy." She glanced at the small fairy, who was sound asleep in the hood of her cloak.

Philip returned Rose's smile, and Theo couldn't help feeling a twinge of jealousy as Philip took Rose's arm and led her down the hall.

I need to stop that, he thought to himself. There was no point getting jealous over Philip's relationship with Rose. Not at the moment, anyway, when Philip was maintaining the pretense of an engagement with Isra, Rose's younger sister. When Philip and Isra admitted the whole thing was a joke, or even a necessary falsehood to protect Isra and Ronan from King Stefanos, *that* would be the time for Theo to worry.

Not that he would worry. Philip was a good man, and a good friend. He would treat Rose well.

Theo frowned at his own thoughts. He should have been more concerned over the situation in Rhone rather than his jealousy.

Since the assassination attempt on King Stefanos' life a few months before, Rose's mother, Queen Leea, had been imprisoned as the prime suspect. Isra and Ronan, also considered a threat, had been able to sneak out of the kingdom safely. They had no place to go—that was, until Isra was inspired to go to Einish and introduce herself as Philip's soon-to-be bride. They were going to meet with Isra and Ronan in a few days in Einish's port city, O'Lin.

"What's wrong?" Ethan asked, as he fell into step with Theo. "Aren't you happy Natala is finally no longer our problem?"

"Oh, I'm happy about that," Theo said. "I was just wondering how Isra and Ronan are doing. I'm glad we are getting closer to seeing them again. Things have not been easy lately."

"When are we going to see them?" Ethan asked. "I'd love to show Isra my skills on the harp. Rose says she's the better musician between them."

"She is," Theo agreed, remembering when they were younger, Isra would delicately pluck at her harp while he bungled about on his. Rose would sit and compare notes with Ronan on how to turn it in a bow before managing a poor rendition of her scales. He smiled; over ten years had passed since then, but he had never forgotten how graceful Rose looked as she played, while she concentrated on her notes.

Ethan rubbed his shoulders, where he had tied his bag back earlier. "My shoulders hurt. I'm glad we can rest here for a few days."

"How are you feeling?" Theo asked. "We'll likely have some time later to train. Would you want to work on your sword skills some more?"

"No," Ethan scoffed. "But I will, because it's training. And this is not vacation."

Theo smirked. "Did you hear Rose say that as we can into the palace?"

"Yes." Ethan grinned.

"I thought as much. You might want to try to make it sound more innocent next time you imitate her. That way she will not realize you're making fun of her."

"Noted."

Theo glanced back up at Rose, just as she glanced back at him.

She hurriedly turned back to Philip. He could hear her asking about supplies, and paid attention to Philip's response long enough to know it was a needless question.

Rose was still avoiding him.

Weeks on the road had not let her forget that moment they shared. Theo felt a rush of satisfaction; it was good to know if he was suffering, he was at least not suffering alone.

Now, he thought, the trick was just to make her suffer enough that she admitted it.

A new voice called from down the hall. "So I hear my younger brother has come to visit, and he didn't feel the need to let me know he had arrived properly."

"Derick!" Philip cried.

Theo watched as Philip turned and hurried to rush over to his brother. It made him miss his own brother, Thad, who was helping their grandfather tend to religious matters back in Rhone's capital city, Havilah.

Philip's blatant devotion to his brother was heartwarming, Theo thought, as he watched his friend embrace the King of Einish and Crystal Lake. The feeling of trust and affection between them was mutual.

"I didn't know you were here," Philip said. "I thought you were with Mother back in Einish."

"I was, for a little while," Derick said. "You've been gone for over half a year, little brother. There are reasons that demand I travel."

"I'm sure Mother is one of the reasons," Philip remarked, his voice jovial.

"Yes, but there are other reasons as well, and, seeing as how they are kingdom business, I will be sure to fill you in on them later." Derick laughed, a full-throated laugh that reminded Theo of Philip.

It was not the only thing about them that was similar. Like Philip, Derick had copper-colored hair, even though it was a slightly darker shade. There were similar lines in their faces, with sharp eyes, and a round boyishness that, without a beard like his brother's, made Derick seem younger.

As the two of them exchanged affectionate barbs, both defending and deriding their mother's habits, Theo remembered Philip telling him that his father had died when he was very young. As he watched the two of them, he had a feeling Derick served as a father figure for Philip as well.

"Is Juliette here with you?" Philip asked. "I'd love for the two of you to meet my new friends."

Derick glanced over Philip's shoulder. "I'd love to meet them now," he said, waving them over. "Juliette is preoccupied, relaxing in one of the natural hot springs."

"I'd forgotten about the Crystal Lake springs," Philip said. He looked up at Derick with a quizzical expression. "Is she well? I know the springs are said to have healing powers."

"Plenty use the hot springs just to relax. But she's more than well," Derick said. "We just found out she's pregnant."

"That's wonderful!" Philip gave Derick another hug. "Congratulations."

"Thank you." Derick gave him a sheepish smile. "We had to try to beat you for good news, I guess. I heard of your own engagement only last week."

"Oh, yes," Philip said. "She's just lovely, Derick. I can't wait for you to meet her."

Derick turned to Rose. "Well, she certainly is beautiful." He graciously bowed to Rose.

Theo might have laughed at the disgust on Rose's face—he knew better than anyone that she hated it when people complimented her on her beauty—if he didn't secretly want to punch Derick himself.

Philip shook his head. "Not this one," he said. "But Princess Rose is the older sister to Princess Isra, my betrothed."

"Oh, well, my apologies, Your Highness," Derick said.

Rose gave him a cool look. "Rose, please," she replied, keeping her tone light. "We are very grateful to be guests in your kingdom, Majesty."

"You are very welcome. Any friends of Phil's are friends of mine," Derick assured her. "Please, feel free to use the castle for whatever you need."

"Thank you," Rose said. "I will."

Theo heard the prim tone in her voice, and he knew Rose would make good on that promise. She would likely be raiding the stables for horses and supplies before the evening came, he thought.

Philip quickly introduced the rest of them to the King. When Theo's turn came, he was surprised when Derick reached out for his hand.

"I've heard about you," he said as Theo shook his hand, accepting the greeting of one solider to another. "I have some traders out in the Romani territory. They've told me about a man who fought the dragon of the Serpent's Garden and lived to tell the tale."

"Hey, that could have been me," Philip stepped in. "I was there, too."

"I was the one who was actually with Rose when she got the dragon's blood," Ethan insisted.

"I almost gouged out his eyes," Philip said.

"That reminds me," Ethan said. "The dragon told me to hit you for that."

"Enough," Rose cut in. "Derick is the one who is talking to Theo. You really shouldn't interrupt, especially when he was the one who saved me from the dragon in the first place."

Theo felt proud, hearing her words.

"I'm sure it wasn't Phil," Derick said. "I would've heard his name for sure if it had been him. They said it was a knight of the highest order."

"Well, thank you," Theo murmured politely. "But I am not officially a knight for the kingdom of Rhone."

"Then you should be knighted here, as a solider for my kingdom," Deric said. "Of course, that's assuming the rumors were true."

Rose stepped forward to stand beside Theo. "Of course it's true. I just said he saved my life. He has the marks on his back to prove it."

"Well, that's settled then," Derick said as he stated retreating down the hall. "I have some meetings to get to, brother, so please excuse me. But come to dinner tonight, and we will feast at my brother's return, and the arrival of the kingdom's newest knight and champion. I'll send out the servants to get you new clothes and anything else you might need."

Derick continued to ramble on for some time, and ended up talking to himself more as he turned the corner.

"Well," Sophia said, "he's nice. But he seems distracted."

"He should be," Philip said. "He's going to be a father soon. And he hasn't been the King of Einish for that long. My mother was regent for several years, before he married Juliette last year."

"Maybe it's Rose's fault," Mary said with a yawn, groggy from a lack of restful sleep and long hours of travel. "He probably got distracted when he saw her."

"That reminds me, I do apologize about his remark," Philip said to Rose. "He has heard more of your legend than anything about Isra. Many people don't realize there are two princesses of Rhone."

"I know." Rose snorted. "Not many people in Rhone know there are two princesses, thanks to the King and Queen. I can hardly blame your brother for not realizing it."

Theo knew from her tone she was still irritated by it, however nicely she tried to hide it. He almost reached for her, but decided against it as Philip came up and placed his arm around Rose's shoulders.

"The world will know the truth soon enough," Philip promised. "And anyway, Isra will still be a princess once you are Queen. So that should be an easy transition for you and Isra."

Rose rolled her eyes. "Let's just get to our rooms," she said. "I'm sure we're all ready to relax for a few hours."

"Just for a few hours," Sophia said with a giggle. "I'm going to see about finding those hot springs he was talking about."

Theo allowed his attention to turn to their surroundings as Philip began answering the questions that came his way. The castle of Crystal Lake strongly reminded him of Rhone's. It was in the classic style, with towers and winding steps. As they were currently walking through the keep, he saw it was furnished with various luxuries and even some fine art from around the world.

They had arrived at the castle just before the midmorning hour, and the fog of the mountains had cleared to reveal a small, but durable castle. It must have undergone quite a few repairs and updates over the years, Theo thought as he allowed himself to reach out and touch one of the hanging tapestries.

His hand stilled and he stepped back, looking up at the full picture.

His eyes widened in shock, and he stopped in his tracks.

"Queen Lucia," he said, awed by the picture before him.

The tapestry was very similar to the one his mother had hung so proudly in their house; the fairy queen looked outward, and he felt as though her eyes, such a pretty mix of green and blue, seemed to stare back at him—seemed to haunt him, the same way his past did.

Theo felt his chest tighten. He remembered that night, when his Uncle Thom had hurried to burn his mother's tapestry. When he had learned his parents were dead and someone had attacked his uncle.

Does this one carry Magdust between its threads, too? Theo wondered as he studied it. He pressed into the fabric, but it was too finely woven for him to detect any Magdust.

"Where's Mary when you need her?" he muttered to himself, sighing as he stepped back. The others were already out of sight. He supposed it was just as well, since Rose was carrying Mary in her traveling cloak's hood.

Theo decided he would have to ask about the tapestry later. It was not only unusual that it was here—the legend of Queen Lucia and her gallant knight, Sir Benedict, who would become the first knight in Rhone, and eventually king as well, was more history of Rhone than it was of either Einish or the kingdom of Crystal Lake—but the idea that it was connected to his past, connected to the illegal Magdust trade, gave him cause for concern.

3

Rose knew she should not let Derick's greeting make her feel alienated, but even if she could disregard that entirely, divorcing it from her memory completely, she knew soon enough that she would have still felt like an outcast.

Dinner was proof enough of that, she thought bitterly. She picked sparingly at her plate, full of foods she didn't recognize. Rose didn't even have time to learn the new foods by their names before some server came around, whipped her plate away, and handed her a new one.

Beside her, Derick and Philip were talking and chatting uproariously, and seeing how much they genuinely adored each other's company, Rose decided it would be unkind to blame that for her loneliness.

The others were eating without complaint—even Natala, Rose noticed, hiding her smile in her cup as she peeked a glance over at the surly guide. Sophia and Ethan were comparing different dishes, while even Mary seemed overly delighted by the pastries.

I should have sat next to Theo. She glanced across the wide table at her best friend, as he sat at Derick's left hand. Theo met her gaze and gave her a look she knew meant he was counting down the time to when he could escape, the same as she was.

There was something else, too, she noticed. There was a distracted quality to him. Something was on his mind.

She caught his eye. "Are you okay?" she mouthed to him.

He nodded, and the he titled his head in Ethan's direction. Rose glanced over just in time to see the younger boy grab a chunk of meat and stuff it into his mouth, before gnawing on it hungrily.

Theo's eyes widened, and then he gave her a half-smile, silently letting her know Ethan seemed to be willing to eat for two of them, or even more, so there was no need for him to be overly excited about dinner.

Rose shrugged back as she smiled, glad she could still talk to Theo, even if with a table between them.

Really the only one who was supposed to be eating for two was Derick's wife, the Queen of Einish and Crystal Lake, who was sitting at the other end of the table. Rose noticed that Juliette didn't seem as interested in food as Ethan.

If anything, Rose thought, the Queen was content to pick at her food as much as Rose was. Rose watched her for a long moment, and then realized that Juliette was probably as lonely as she was, given that Derick was preoccupied with Philip, and she didn't know anyone else.

At least I have Theo to exchange silent half-conversations, Rose thought.

It was then that Rose realized Philip and Derick's conversation had grown softer.

She leaned over carefully, under the guise of reaching for her cup, straining her ears to hear.

" … there are some issues that the people wanted addressed, so that's why I came here." Derick's voice seemed to grow even softer as he added, "I didn't want Juliette's people to worry, and I didn't want her to worry, either."

"I can understand," Philip replied. "We can check things out for you. We'll be headed in that direction before too long."

"I'm hoping that even though I know you are in a hurry to get back to Rhone, you'll be able to get some idea of how to solve it. I can send some troops with you, if you are willing to lead them."

"I'll ask Rose about it. She might prefer them to come after us, just to make sure we didn't miss anything."

"I don't want to impose on Her Highness."

Rose could not stand it any longer. "What's happening?" she asked.

Philip jerked around awkwardly, before clearing his throat. "Well, Derick, you do know of Rose's reputation. She might be able to do something."

Derick hesitated. "Okay. I guess it's okay to talk business over dinner."

"It's really alright," Philip insisted. "You know our mother is not here to object."

Derick nodded. "More true words were never spoken," he said. "If you say so, little brother."

"There's no one more reliable than Rose," Philip declared. "You can count on that."

Rose shifted in her seating, trying to keep the annoyance out of her face as much as she tried to keep her long skirts from keeping her in her chair. "Tell me."

"I mentioned earlier that there was some kingdom business that had called me to Crystal Lake Palace," Derick said. "It seems that there has been a surge in the illegal Magdust trade, between the border of Crystal Lake and Einish."

Rose felt her heart sink. "The small area of the border you share with Rhone?"

Derick nodded. "I intended to take this up with King Stefanos," he admitted. "But seeing as you are here, and you are the heir to the kingdom, I guess there's no harm in informing you."

"I know there has been an increase in the trade since last year," Rose said. "That was part of the reason my father wanted me to come home from my travels before. He says Magdalina's fairies are getting bolder; I know there has been trouble since the fairyfolk in Rhone had fallen under Magdalina's rule many years ago."

She did not want to mention that the rise in crime was likely due to her eighteenth birthday approaching, the recent attempt on King Stefanos' life, and the resulting imprisonment of her mother. The kingdom morale had to be significantly low lately, Rose thought.

She was still determined to get back to her mother and find the villain who tried to poison her father, but she knew that Magdalina's curse still remained her first priority.

It had to, she told herself. Once the curse was broken, , Rose knew her kingdom would once more have the confidence they needed.

It was hard not to think that it might be better to go and settle the kingdom issues first, especially since she was so close to seeing her brother and sister again. There was no point in being free of her curse if she had no kingdom to rule when she got back from Magdalina's castle in the Darkwood Forest.

Everything took time, Rose thought bitterly.

"That must be why they have expanded their trade alliance into my kingdom," Derick said, making Rose return her full attention to their conversation.

"Rhone has long made the trade illegal," Rose assured him. "We have done what we could to stop the spread of it. The Magdust trade is such a horrendous topic in itself. The idea that it might be spreading is dreadful."

ONCE UPON A PRINCESS

"I agree. I was going to go and inspect the forest once more later on this week," he said. "I've had several scouting reports come in on the location of the trade alliance. So far I know there is a smaller group of traders who are using the Wandering Caverns as a base; it is a larger cave near the border, only a few hours from O'Lin."

"If you can get us a map," Rose said, "I'm sure we can take care of it. Ethan is our map reader, and I have yet to find a fairy that can defeat me as long as I have Queen Lucia's sword." She brightened at the thought of getting a chance to use her newly acquired ruby, the one that held the dragon's blood.

"I would be in your debt for taking care of this for me." Derick leaned back in his chair.

"Consider it a dowry of sorts," Rose said, giving Philip a smirk.

"We have a deal then," Derick said. He called over a servant and began whispering to him, calling for a written agreement to be drawn up, while Philip turned to her.

"Maybe you should have offered our services as a form of payment rather than a gift," Philip said.

"Nonsense," Rose said. "We have done more for less."

"I meant for Natala's room and board," Philip told her, nudging her shoulder.

Rose smothered her own laughter as she saw the woman, half-asleep, as she used her plate as a pillow. "I don't think your brother has enough problems for me to work off her debt."

"You don't have to work off any debt at all," Philip said. "I was just teasing. Or maybe pointing out that he would do better for a promise of a real and likely high debt, rather than a dowry he won't be able to use. My mother would be the one you should discuss the dowry with anyway."

Rose arched her brow. "We'll see," she said. "In the meantime, you should finish your dinner. We're going to start getting ready to leave. I don't want to stay here for longer than another day or two. If the Magdust trade in on the rise, I don't think I'll have time to bring it down and save my mother."

"I'll have the servants start working on preparing for our journey to Einish," Philip promised. "But maybe you should take your own advice. You've barely touched your food, and this is truly Einish's finest. My brother likes to eat well, and he's no doubt doubled down since Juliette is pregnant. Take some time to eat, drink, and refresh yourself, Rose."

Rose sighed. She did not want to explain to Philip why she was unable to eat. She just shrugged. "I think I'm tired," she finally said.

"While the servants get our stuff together, you should rest," Philip said. "Crystal Lakes is a great place to unwind. People come here from all over the continent to enjoy the nearby hot springs. There are some that are connected to the castle, just for the people here."

"Sure, sure. I'll consider it." Rose nodded, before as her attention turned to Theo once more. That brooding, contemplative look was on his face once more.

She wanted to find out what he was worried about. It was no good for them to be worried about different things, and she had more than enough problems to deal with.

But everything takes time, Rose reminded herself, as she headed off to her own rooms. She needed some of that time to herself.

ONCE UPON A PRINCESS

4

It was two days later when Theo paced around the small chapel, trying to find his focus. He had risen early—easy enough to do, after only a few hours of troubled sleep.

After considering his options, he had made his way down to the chapel, hoping God would answer his prayers more quickly if he went out to meet him.

The palace was nearly still, as most of the servants were still asleep, or they were sentries tending to the night watch. There was only one monk in the chapel beside him, who had taken one look at Theo, no doubt noticing his plain tunic and commoner's pants, before he dismissed him.

It is not like I am a threat to this place, Theo thought, as he sat down in one of the benches and bowed his head.

His prayers were silent and private, some of his own inner musings insisting on staying a secret even from himself.

Despite his desire for revenge against Everon, Magdalina's son, for slaying his parents, Theo knew that he had cause to be thankful for all the good things in his life. He might have been torn from another life—one where he had a mother and a father, and a home of their own. He knew his path to knighthood was unconventional, but he was grateful for Philip's brother to grant him such a high recognition.

Maybe even King Stefanos, who had always seemed at odds with Theo, would grant him the same privilege when they arrived back in Rhone.

Theo let out a small sigh. There were so many questions he had about the King, about Rose, about his family, and about his future. Their answers never seemed to come to him.

He opened his eyes as the monk came up next to him. "What troubles your soul?"

Theo hesitated. "Too much," he replied. "Too much worry and despair."

"Have you confessed your sins?"

Theo nodded, deciding not to let the man know he had yet to repent of all of them.

The monk nodded. "Our Heavenly Father hears your prayers. As your sins have been washed away, so may your worries. Let not your heart be troubled by your concerns, but continue to trust and have faith in that which sustains us all." He rested his hand on Theo's shoulder for a moment, before he began walking away.

"Thank you, Brother," Theo murmured. He crossed his arms and leaned back against the wooden pew. At the sudden pressure, he felt his back ache, the wounds from the dragon suddenly tender. He groaned and sat up.

"If you would like, sir," the monk spoke up, "the Crystal Lake hot springs are available for your use. A special room in the bottom of the castle leads out to a nearby pool. You might want to consider it if you are searching for peace. Even our Lord knew when to rest."

Theo nodded. From the monk's tone, he had to wonder if he was being told to leave. When the monk started to rearrange the ornaments on the altar, Theo decided it was best to slip out. Having been forced to clean and keep the sanctuary back in Rhone's capital city, Theo knew that it was always easier to care for the church when it was empty, and considering the early hour of the morning, he would not be surprised to find he had disrupted the monk with his company.

Besides, the hot springs actually sound like a good idea. Theo wondered if the rumors about the waters and their healing powers were true, and if the waters would do anything for his wounds.

With the help of some of the palace guards, Theo was able to find the stairway leading beneath the castle. The winding hallway ended with a grand door, with only one guard on duty. Theo nodded to the man, who remained silent as he stepped to the side and allowed him to pass.

Once he opened the door, and found himself alone on the other side of it, Theo felt his mouth drop open at the stunning surroundings. The room opened up into a tall, well-lit atrium, where the sky was hidden by the high ceiling of a cave. The floor gradually transformed into sand, and then gradually gave way to ashen waters, while the soft reflection of the lantern light danced on the surface ripples.

He knew the hot springs were a natural phenomenon in some countries, where heat escaped from underground volcanic pockets.

He breathed in deeply, tasting the moist air, as it intermingled with sulfur and other minerals. He coughed at the unusual taste, and smiled as the sound of it echoed across the large room.

Grateful to be alone, Theo stripped down to his linens, tossing the rest of his garments on one of the cave's proud stalagmites, before he slowly sank into the waters.

Immediately, the wounds on his back ached with pained pleasure. The warmth of the water seeped into each scar, tearing at the sensitive skin even while soothing it.

Sweat collected on his forehead as he moved slowly through the waters, Theo had to admit he was glad the monk had suggested going to the hot springs.

The water grew deeper as he moved away from the pool's entrance. His feet dug into the gritty mud as he made his way to the far edge of the pool, toward a small niche, where the cave wall rounded against the shadows.

The other day, Ethan had told him that when they went down to the springs, Sophia and Mary had found some natural deposits, where there were piles of cream-like substance in some of the alcoves. It was supposed to be good for scars, and while Theo was not concerned with how his back looked, he did not want Rose to be upset at the sight of it.

Not that Rose would be upset because of how they looked, Theo thought, recalling how she had helped bandage him up several times on the road from the Romani territory.

But he knew she felt responsible for his pain, even though he had willingly protected her; he could see the guilt in her eyes each time, and he was getting less of a chance to displace her shame as she avoided him. Anything he could do to remove her guilt seemed like a worthwhile pursuit.

Just as he found a small pile of cream tucked just underneath the water, he heard the door to the hot springs open and slam shut.

He glanced over, ready to call out his welcome to whoever it was. He immediately faltered, stunned by what he saw.

Rose had pushed off her leggings and pulled off her tunic when he had caught sight of her. She was wearing only her undergarments, the white linen hanging delicately over her toned body. He could see her soft curves, usually hidden by her knight's armor; his eyes followed the flare of her hips. The lantern light landed on the delicate skin of her legs, touching her in places he could only envy. As if his thoughts had finally shocked him enough to return to reality, Theo turned away and ducked further into the alcove. He did not need to look at his reflection in the water to know his face was flushed over, colored a deep scarlet.

ONCE UPON A PRINCESS

What is she doing here? Theo wondered. *Why would she come in this place, and why now?*

The heat of the waters seemed to increase drastically, as he heard Rose slip into the water. When he heard her release a small sigh of pleasure at the water's embrace, Theo had to squeeze his eyes shut and bury his face in his hands.

He shook his head and hurriedly wiped it off; it was the absolute worst time to get anything in his eyes, if he was going to try to sneak past Rose before she discovered him.

If that's the only option I have, he thought to himself.

He glanced back toward her, relieved to see Rose had found a place to sit and stew, close to the water's edge. He was supremely grateful to see that her eyes were closed. Theo began to move slowly, not wanting to rouse her from her meditative position.

But once he realized he was safely out of her sight, for the moment, Theo gave into temptation to look at her. She was sitting with the water up to her neck, with her hair bound up in a high bun; several tendrils of shortened length escaped the tie and curled at the heat. He could see the porcelain skin of her shoulders peeking out of the gentle waters. He could see the linen of her undergarments, as they bubbled up from the pressure of the underwater springs.

Theo took another few steps forward. He was careful to slip off to the side, standing far off to the side of Rose. As he neared the edge of the water near the door, he realized that he might be able to get out of the pool without Rose's notice, but he would have a harder time leaving the room. She was relaxing right beside the stalagmite where he'd thrown his things earlier.

He was no longer able to move without possibly disturbing her. He tried to think of a way not to terrify her when he stepped on a sharp rock and lost his balance. He stumbled around in the pool as he quickly regained his balance.

Theo felt his breath suck in as the water rippled stridently across the pool. He hoped beyond all hope Rose did not hear the noise.

When Rose's eyes snapped opened, and she whirled around, he knew he was in trouble.

For a split second, all they did was stare at each other. And then Rose screamed and began scrambling to get away.

"Theo!" she yelled, sending the hot water flying as she hurriedly moved away from him. "What do you think are you doing here?!"

"I'm sorry," he called back, trying to shield himself from her splashing. "I was just relaxing, I swear. I promise didn't see anything."

"I don't believe you," Rose yelled, as she shoved another wave of water at him.

"Rose, please stop," he shouted. "It was an accident."

She crossed her arms, sinking all the way into the water. There was a look of unmatched fury on her face as she glared at him from just above the water's surface. "What … are … you … doing … here?" she repeated, her teeth grinding out each word, letting him know she was more than livid.

"I couldn't sleep," he said. "So I came here. I thought it would be good on my back."

"Why didn't you tell me you were here when I came in?" she grumbled.

"I didn't hear you until … " Theo let his voice trail off as he thought of seeing her bared flesh, the fair ivory of her legs and the strong muscles of her arms.

Rose sent another splash flying at him, this time striking his face.

"Ouch!" His eyes burned at the mixture of the hot water and natural minerals. "What was that for?"

"For lying," Rose snapped.

He could tell from the direction of her voice and the streaming water sounds she had stepped out of the water. Theo glared in her direction. "I wasn't lying."

"I can tell by looking at you!" she yelled. "Your face is all red."

"It's really warm in here, if you haven't noticed," Theo argued back. But he didn't want to admit that she was right; he had seen more than enough to make her feel uncomfortable. "It's just the temperature in here, that's all."

"I still don't believe you."

"Come on, Rose, you can trust me."

"I don't know about that anymore," Rose said angrily.

"If I wanted to look," Theo said, his own temper getting the better of him, "I wouldn't have come forward. I wouldn't have said anything."

He stopped trying to brush away the burning in his eyes, as he realized how cruel he sounded. He heard her inhale sharply, and instantly he regretted his words. "Rose … "

She went quiet, and he could tell she was distracted.

"You know what? It doesn't matter," Rose said. "I'm sorry for splashing you, I suppose, but at least this way I know you can't see me now."

Theo groaned. "Didn't you ask the guard if there was anyone here before you came in?" he asked. "What if there were others?"

"I didn't see a guard," Rose shot back, her tone sharp, even if her voice was muffled. "And I didn't think anyone would be here. This is really early in the morning, you know."

"Yes," he said. "I know. Did you have trouble sleeping?"

ONCE UPON A PRINCESS

"There are so many things to do," Rose replied in a non-committal tone. "I don't have time to answer all your questions. I'm leaving."

He finished wiping the water from his eyes. He was still blinking furiously when he saw she had her shirt on once more.

For all the good it did, he thought. The hot springs had added a flush to her legs, and the wetness of her skin ensured that her shirt clung to her body. He had a hard time ignoring how short her shirt was. How one sleeve hung off one of her shoulders.

How much he wanted her to be his.

He stopped moving toward her, his body still half-sunk in the hot springs.

Rose held her tunic and her other clothes against her tightly, still having trouble looking him in the eye. "I'm leaving," she repeated. "You can stay. You're probably right that the water would be good for your injuries. I don't need it as much as you do."

"Rose," he said, as she headed toward the door. "It *was* an accident."

"It doesn't matter," she murmured, but he knew she was lying. She gripped handle on the door, and hurriedly disappeared on the other side.

Theo felt awful as she left. They were already having problems when it came to communicating. *This isn't going to make it any better,* he thought.

He sank back into the water, alone once more, letting the hot springs massage their comfort into his back. Time passed, slowly and quietly.

Despite the physical comfort, Theo could only grimace.

ONCE UPON A PRINCESS

But on the very small bright side, he thought reluctantly, he certainty had something else to occupy his thoughts.

ONCE UPON A PRINCESS

5

Rose hurried down the hall, tugging her tunic over her head while trying to juggle her boots. She had wriggled into the rest of her clothes as soon as the door to the underground springs had closed, but the moment she could leave, she did.

How dare he! How dare he sit there and act like nothing had happened.

Her heart was still racing, as her mind screamed with humiliation and, she cursed herself, excitement. The thought of what had just happened angered her as much as it embarrassed her.

The rough texture of her shirt rubbed against her wet skin, as she nimbly finished tying her belt. Her feet, still bare, flinched at the uneven flooring of the castle, but she did not slow her pace.

She vowed that she would not think of seeing Theo, seeing him in his wet undergarments, fighting off her watery blows as he tried to calm her.

It was not the first time she had seen his chest or his back, but something about the way he had been covered with the steam of the hot springs, and the way the light had flickered off his chest....

"No!" she admonished herself. "No, stop thinking about it! This is *exactly* what you know you cannot do!"

Rose was relieved that she was still alone as she hurried through the castle. She knew they had guards keeping watch, but she had been lucky enough to avoid them.

In fact, she suddenly realized as she looked around, she was lost.

"How stupid can you be?" she asked, chastising herself. Rose looked around the unfamiliar halls of the palace, uncertain of where she had made a wrong turn. "Great."

She took a few moments to put her boots on, and then tried to recall her steps. Invariably, she had to stop herself from thinking of everything that happened before she left the hot springs.

Finally, she saw a familiar marker.

The tapestry of Queen Lucia hung proudly against the cold stone of the castle walls. The penetrating eyes seemed harrowing as they gazed down at her. Rose watched as the first gleam early morning light—or maybe the last of the moonlight—as it illuminated the Queen's gaze.

From where Rose stood, she saw a look of quiet judgment, almost a motherly look of sorts. It was as if Lucia knew of the dark secrets of her heart, the ones that she might have sung to the dragon, but still tried to silence inside her own heart.

"It's a lovely tapestry, don't you think?"

Rose didn't move as Juliette came and stood beside her. "It was a wedding gift from one of our ambassadors who lives in Einish."

"It is beautiful," Rose said, as she stared at it. She didn't feel the need to admit it made her unnerved.

"There aren't many of these tapestries in the world anymore," Juliette said. "The lady who made them died several years ago. She was a very skilled weaver. She used to work at some of the tournaments around the Einish border near Rhone."

"What happened to her?" Rose asked, more concerned with establishing rapport with the new Queen than finding out more about the weaver's fate.

ONCE UPON A PRINCESS

"She fell in love with one of Rhone's knights, from what I heard, much to her father's dismay. It wasn't too long before they married and had children."

Rose felt an uncomfortable amount of jealousy at the woman's happiness.

"The tapestries of Lucia are thought to have magical powers," Juliette continued. "Of course, I don't believe that. But when you see it, there are moments when you have to wonder if it's not true."

Rose nodded. "I will agree with that," she said. "I've met Titania, Lucia's daughter who lives out in the Greek territories, near the Aegean. This picture reminds me of her."

"Lucia was known for her charms, before they ended up costing her."

"Titania told me that she made Benedict, one of King Arthur's wandering knights, a knight of Rhone. He became King after he managed to dispose of her."

Juliette giggled. "There's always more to the story," she said. "In the version of their story I have heard, Benedict and Lucia, coming from their different worlds, had trouble deciding how to rule the people of Rhone. Benedict had the advantage in war; Lucia had her fairy power. He wanted to rule through force, and she wanted to rule by magic. He went along with pleasing her for a long time, but as it grew harder not to feel like her equal, her partner, and even her king, he used Magdust to gain power."

"And that's why he imprisoned her?" Rose asked. "Because she wouldn't bow down to his wishes?"

Juliette smiled. "Have you ever been in love, Princess?"

Rose felt the familiar fury at the question, but she knew Juliette was asking it out of ignorance, not to make her feel bad.

"No," she answered. "And please, call me Rose."

"It might be hard for you understand. Love between two people almost has a life of its own. Some poets have compared it to dancing, where there is a give and take, a leader and a follower. Other philosophers have said that it's more like a sword fight."

"I'll take that one over the dancing," Rose said. She grinned. "I'm better at fighting."

"With all the fighting you've done, from the tales I've heard, you should know that there is a time for peace."

"Of course." Rose nodded.

"It is the same in marriage, when two people are in love. Sometimes one person leads, and the other must submit." Juliette sighed. "I don't think either Lucia or Benedict were able to handle the submission part that comes with love."

"I don't blame them," Rose scoffed. "It's a sign of losing."

"When you truly love someone, it is more a sign of trust." Juliette smiled. "When Benedict had to earn her love, I imagine it was very hard for him to trust her. What if he wasn't able to keep hold of her affection? That was why it was easier to dispose of her in the end. If it wasn't for the matter of the kingdom, he likely would have just left her."

Rose looked back up at the Queen, and suddenly she saw her sad, judgmental eyes in a new light; Lucia suddenly came across as too proud, too stubborn, and too aloof. She never had to earn Benedict's love, but she was free to be the judge of whether or not he was worthy of her.

"Well," Rose said, after a few long moments of silence, "I guess either way you look at it, at least the tapestry is beautiful."

"Beautiful things can hide ugly secrets," Juliette said. Rose cringed, thinking of her own heart, hidden by her outward charms. "But you're right about the tapestry."

"Do you come down here to look at it a lot, or did you just happen to be passing by when you found me?" Rose asked, happy to find a way to change the subject. She did not want to think about true love and marriage, real or legendary.

"I usually wake up early to say goodbye to the moonlight," Juliette admitted. "Even though it has been over a year since the sorcerer who enchanted me was killed, I fear I will wake up to find this has all been a dream, and I will turn back into a swan at moonset."

"I can tell you it's not a dream," Rose told her. "If that makes you feel better."

Juliette giggled again, making Rose wonder how young she was. She seemed very innocent. Derick was a few years older than Philip, but Rose had a hard time imagining that Juliette was much older than she was, if Juliette was older at all.

"There's just so much in my life I couldn't believe before," Juliette said. "I mean, not too many people end up cursed."

"Tell me about it," Rose muttered.

"And now, here I am," Juliette continued, oblivious to Rose's increasing discomfort, "pregnant, with a husband who loves me, and a stronger kingdom coming out of our two lands. It is a miracle."

"See?" Rose said. She gave the Queen a kind and sad smile. "If it's a miracle, then it's not a dream."

"I'll take comfort in your observation, Rose," Juliette said, her eyes lit up with happiness. "And I thank you for it."

"You're welcome."

Rose shifted her feet uncomfortably as Juliette put a hand on her belly, where, inside of her, her child grew. Rose did not want to think about how much she envied Juliette.

"Speaking of observations, Juliette," Rose said, deciding it was time to change the subject once more, "I was wondering

ONCE UPON A PRINCESS

if you would be able to point me in the direction of my room? I seem to be a bit lost."

"Sure," Juliette replied.

Despite Juliette's kindness, Rose was glad, moments later, to be free from the Queen's presence. *And that,* she told herself, *is why I don't want to get married.*

Juliette was a very lovely lady, and Rose was sure she was a nice person. But what did she really know of the world? Of another's suffering? Juliette was just a pretty queen who could empower the nation by having children. Rose doubted Juliette would ever play a real, decisive role in her nation's future again, and she even suspected that Juliette would not mind if that were the case.

Rose tried not to sigh. It was also possible Juliette would not even notice her secondary role. Juliette would just do what she had been talking about earlier; she would see it as part of a loving marriage, and submit.

Rose frowned. She knew she certainty had no desire to do that.

But as she approached the door to her room, she knew she was not being completely honest with herself.

Theo was standing outside her door.

The sight of him, fully dressed, with his hair still sticky with steam and sweat, caused a pool of heat to settle into her belly. Her mind was flooded with that moment back in Poiyana, when she *had* surrendered, when she *had* submitted—when she had closed her eyes and waited for Theo to kiss her.

Not only had she wanted it, she had willingly hoped for it.

Rose watched as Theo raised his hand to knock on her door, and waited again. She realized he did not see her in the shadows of the hall behind him. He thought she was already back in her room.

He faltered just as his hand poised to knock.

Rose held her breath. Her whole body went rigid as she watched him, wondering if he was going to knock on her door.

She wondered, if she were on the other side of the door, if she would open it.

Slowly, eventually, Theo dropped his hand.

He ran his hand through his ebony hair and then shook his head. He slowly backed away, before he headed down the hall in the other direction. He never saw her.

The instant he was out of sight, Rose hurried into her room, suddenly distraught. The heat in her belly cooled into nausea, and she felt dizzy.

Rose was not fooled; she knew the answer to her question. She had wanted him to knock, and she wanted to believe that she would have answered. Part of her wanted to go find him again and tell him what she was thinking.

Rose fell back against the door, the rough wood. "No, no. That's stupid. I'm not going to say anything."

"Not going to say anything about what?"

Mary's voice, rested and relaxed, so much at odds with her own reality, jarred against Rose's exasperation.

Rose looked over toward the small fairy, who was lying down on one of the bigger pillows on her bed.

"What's wrong, Rose?" Mary asked, sitting up.

Rose shook her head. "Nothing," she insisted. "How are you feeling? Did you get enough rest?"

Mary glowered at her. "I'd be better," she said, "if I knew you weren't lying. Tell me what's wrong."

Rose felt the heat in the back of her neck. "I don't want to talk about it, Mary. It's too embarrassing."

"I could always do a truth spell," Mary mused.

"Now I know you're teasing me." Rose gave her a small smile. "I know you would never betray me."

"Rose." Mary sat up against the fluffy pillows. "I'm worried for you."

"Please, don't worry about me right now. We have a lot prepping to do before we leave tomorrow."

"Rose," Mary said. "Come and lie down. Your cheeks are flushed and your eyes are glassy. You're feverish." Her wings, thin and delicate against the last shadow of night, fluttered. She held up her hand against Rose's forehead.

"Little mother," Rose murmured, giving Mary a pat on the head, ruffling the short ginger locks affectionately.

"Let me help you sleep, Rose," Mary said. "You'll feel better. After all the weeks on the road, you need to get some quality sleep. I can attest to the comfort King Derick has been kind enough to offer us. I've barely wanted to move since we've come."

"I know you needed it," Rose said. "After all the healing you've done for Theo, I'm well aware you needed it. I know it took a lot out of you, fighting against the dragon magic."

Saying his name was a mistake. Rose took another deep breath to steady herself.

"I might be rested, but you're the one who needs it now, Rose."

"No. I'm too afraid of what I might dream of," Rose told her.

"You know, you never did tell me the full story what happened back in the Serpent's Garden," Mary said. "But I never thought it was that terrifying to you.

"I sang to the dragon," Rose reminded her. "I told you that."

"It wasn't just singing," Mary pushed. "I know you, Rose. I've watched over you since the day you were born. Something has changed, and you won't tell me what it is."

"It's awful." Rose pressed against the door, allowing herself to slide down to the floor, her head falling to her chest. More of her hair escaped the quick bun she had tied back earlier.

"I know you have had a hard life, but I have been there more often than not," Mary said. "Let me help you, Rose."

"You can't," Rose told her. "It's me. I'm the problem."

Mary looked at her with an expectant look.

"It's less than six months until my birthday. I don't have much longer."

"We're getting there, Rose."

"I still want so much more out of life." Rose sighed. "I am grateful for you, and the others. I just want … more." She felt the lump in her throat tighten again. "When I went to go see the dragon, and I sang, I sang Queen Lucia's song. About how she wanted love, someone who would be worthy of her love."

"Is that what you want?" Mary asked.

It was harder to answer, now that she knew more about Queen Lucia and her complicated relationship with Benedict.

"Yes. No. I don't know." Rose shook her head. "I'm not worthy of love, Mary. Not really. I'm cursed. I can't offer someone a future, or a family. Not until the curse is broken. I just want the curse broken, so I can be free."

"I think someone will love you even if your curse can't be broken," Mary told her softly.

"I don't want someone to love me like that. Like this," Rose said. "I do have to kill Magdalina if she refuses to free me from her curse, remember? I have to destroy her, to save myself."

ONCE UPON A PRINCESS

"You will be protecting the rest of your family, and likely others, from her wrath," Mary said.

"Even though that's likely true, there is the matter that if I don't make it, anyone who loves me will be devastated." Rose sniffed. "Magdalina has to be the cruelest person who ever lived, to make me suffer like this."

"She was very adamant about making your father pay," Mary remarked. "It seems she did a good job of that."

"Why? What did she want the King to pay for?" Rose asked. "She couldn't have been that upset, just because she was not invited to my party."

"It wasn't just that she was not invited," Mary said. "Everything that could have been done to shield you from her was done. The King didn't even want her to know of your birth."

"Why?" Rose asked. "Why was he afraid of her?"

"I don't know for sure," Mary said. "I heard him talk about breaking a deal with her once. That was it. I didn't hear any details. And that might not even be why she's so upset with him, really."

Rose thought of Theo again. "He hates Theo, too, doesn't he?"

"The King never liked him, precisely because you did," Mary said. "He was upset with him for telling you the truth about your curse, and all the resulting grievances you gave him. You were a perfect child, Rose, before you found out about everything. Once you knew the truth—"

"I was never the same." Rose put her head in her hands. "And the King blames Theo for that."

Mary nodded. "He didn't like that you demanded that Theo would join you and your siblings for classes, either. He felt he should have stayed in the church and let his family take care of educating him. You were lucky you insisted, Rose, or you might not have Theo by your side today."

"I'm the one who's letting him pursue his revenge," Rose said. "Theo might be more lucky if I hadn't."

"Life is never free of pain, Rose," Mary said softy. "But we each get to choose what kind of pain we experience."

"Sometimes it's not a choice," Rose said, thinking how Theo just stood there, in the hot springs, as he looked at her with that strange expression on his face. She wanted to go back to that moment and reach for him instead of run from him, back to that moment when her heart had fluttered so dangerously. "I would never choose this."

"No one would choose to be cursed as you, Rose," Mary said, patting her hand.

Rose nearly jumped. "Yeah," she agreed, her voice listless.

She decided not to correct Mary. She could not imagine confessing her dreams of letting herself fall in love, without fear that the fall would lead to only despair.

There was nothing to be done, Rose thought, desolate once more. She would just go on, as she had always gone on.

"Mary?" Rose looked over at her longtime friend. "It's morning. Let's go over what we need to take care of before we leave here tomorrow. Derick and Philip wanted us to take care of some trouble while we travel through the forest."

"Rose," Mary said, "please, go to bed. You need to rest. You're exhausted. I'll see to everything today."

"No. There's so much to do still. There are so many questions to answer." Rose shook her head, but as soon as she stood up, the room began to spin.

She barely realized she was still awake as Mary whisked her off her feet. The last thing she heard herself say was, "Please don't let me dream, Mary," before there was nothing but darkness.

ONCE UPON A PRINCESS

6

It was hours later when Rose finally stirred from her slumber. The call to wake up came as she felt the easy pressure of a wet rag on her forehead.

"Stop it, Theo," she murmured, waving him away. "I'm fine. See? I'm awake."

"You might be fine, but you're definitely not awake," Philip said, "if you can't see that it's me, instead of Theo."

Rose opened her eyes and rubbed them. "He's the one who usually takes care of me," she heard herself say.

"He passed that duty along to me today, then," Philip assured her as he dabbed her forehead with a dry cloth this time. "He said that you would want to leave the moment you got up, so it would be best if he took care to get everything ready."

Rose stiffened, wondering if Theo had told Philip about what had happened down in the hot springs. She studied Philip's face carefully, trying to see if he was hiding anything from her.

"What?" he asked. "What is it?"

When she decided that Philip's handsome face was innocent enough, she sat up against her pillows.

"I told you sleep would help you, Rose," Mary said. Rose looked over to see Mary was sitting by the window. The thick curtains were drawn back some, allowing the full light of the afternoon to pour into the room.

"So we're going to leave today?" Rose asked, as she pushed past Philip and her covers. She hurried to look outside.

Mary chuckled. "Not as soon as Natala is."

49

Rose breathed a sigh of relief as she looked down at the courtyard below, where Theo was indeed giving a cranky Natala some assistance as she climbed up onto a horse. Even from where she was, she could hear Natala's groaning complaints and screechy interrogations.

"It's too hot to travel today. I'll be dead by nightfall. Did you make sure to pack me plenty of blankets? I'll need them when it gets cold. I can tell it's going to get cold tonight. I'll probably die freezing. I can't believe this is the best horse you were able to get for me. I thought this was a king's palace?"

Natala whirled around as she sat on the horse, making sure the ropes holding up her packs, many of which clearly had blankets inside, before pinching her mouth into her favorite frown.

Theo took her hand, giving her a gallant bow, a farewell worthy of a true lady. Rose smiled at his kindness. There was no way Natala was even close to being a lady.

"I hope your brother doesn't mind she's taking a horse," Rose said, turning back to Philip.

"Believe me, Derick was fine parting with it, once he knew it would get rid of her more quickly," Philip said. "When I told him of her temper and her shrewish ways, he didn't hesitate to give into most of her demands."

"Most?" Rose asked. She grinned. "What did he deny her?"

"A lot of money," Philip replied.

Rose laughed as the door opened, and Sophia came inside. "Figures," she said.

"What's funny?" Sophia was carrying a large bundle in her arms. She carried it over to Rose's bed and set it down, her nimble fingers already unraveling the bundle's ties.

"Natala's leaving," Philip said. "I was just telling Mary and Rose about all the money she'd tried to get out of my brother."

Sophia shook her head. "She would have been smarter to ask for a guard," she said. "If she's not taking anyone back, all of her bags will just make her an easier target for thieves."

"Maybe I should send Lannister back with her," Rose said. Of all the members of the group, Lannister, one of the royal guards assigned to protect her, was the only one who had been able to get along with Natala on the way to Crystal Lake. "They did have similar tastes when it came to their choice of beverage."

"Roderick and Captain Locke would probably be okay with that," Mary said. "I've overheard them complaining about how he has not been carrying his weight lately."

Rose was tempted to say she was okay with all of them escorting Natala back to Poiyana, but she had grown more fond of Roderick since their adventures on the island of Maltia. He had proven himself to be her mother's champion while they were there.

He was also mostly quiet and kept to himself the majority of the time, so it wasn't like she had to worry about ordering him around. Captain Locke was content with his duties and his silence as well. Rose knew she had an honorable captain for her guard.

"We could do without Lannister," Rose said. "I would prefer it, as much trouble as she is, that she doesn't go back alone."

"Ethan told me that she had a few people ready to leave for Greece," Philip said. "She's meeting them in the town square today. So I wouldn't worry about her. She seems pretty smart. I suspect if she hides it only if she knows she'll be able to swindle more out of people by playing the victim or the shrew."

"Or both," Rose mused.

"If she's made it this long without one of her passengers letting her get too drunk to avoid walking off a cliff, I suppose I'm not giving her enough credit," Sophia replied.

"Or throwing her off the cliff," Rose muttered.

"Rose," Mary said.

"Hey, you were asleep way more than I was," Rose defended herself. "She was a terror, Mary. While you slept she was constantly on our nerves."

"Speaking of which," Philip said, "you need to make sure you are getting enough rest, Rose. Mary was terrified when you collapsed earlier."

"I did not collapse." Rose willed herself to believe it as much as she wanted the rest of them to believe it.

Sophia rolled her eyes, regardless of the confidence of Rose's assertion. "Come here and check your sword, Rose. Let me make sure it's ready for you before we leave."

"Seriously," Philip said, "you do need to take care of yourself, Rose, and that includes sleep. I don't want to go and meet your brother and sister in Einish only to have to explain to them why you keep falling asleep at the most random times."

"Do you seriously care more about what Isra and Ronan think than what I do?" Rose put her hands on her hips while Sophia ran a rag over the ruby at the hilt of Rose's sword.

"Of course," Philip said. "I promised Isra I would watch out for you while we were away. I don't want to fail her."

"I'm curious," Rose said. "Did she *make* you promise that, or did you gallantly offer to be my babysitter?"

Philip seemed to realize that he might have said too much. "Come on," he said. "That's being unfair, Rose."

"Here," Sophia said, handing Rose her sword. "Check its balance for me, please."

Rose held out the sword straight ahead, teasing Philip enough by leveling it at him while he stood by her bed. "I have a right to ask you about the relationship you have with Isra," she insisted. "After all, she's your betrothed now."

"Not officially," Mary said. "Even if Rose signs the contract, King Stefanos still has to approve it. We haven't heard anything from Rhone for weeks now. Besides, Isra is too young to get married at only sixteen."

"Let's hope the King's still holed up in his room, paranoid and sick," Sophia said. "If Rose can take over the duties of the crown, it'll be easier to convince Magdalina we're not to be trifled with."

"I won't argue with you there," Rose said, "but I don't want to mutiny against my father. It would set a poor precedent for future generations."

"Rose, give the sword a few practice swings," Sophia instructed, interrupting Rose's conversation with Philip again.

"But at least you could okay things of that nature, such as your sister's marriage," Philip said. "That would be easier."

"Is that what you want?" Rose asked.

Before he could answer, there was a knock at the door. Rose's heart beat wildly, remembering how she had felt earlier, seeing Theo outside her door.

"Who is it?" Mary called.

Rose instantly recognized the voice on the other side of the door as one of the many guards. "His Majesty has called for Prince Philip."

"Well, I will go and see him at once, then," Philip replied. "I will have to take my leave. I'm glad to see you're feeling better, Rose, and I will make it my duty to make sure you get more sleep, more consistently, from now on."

Rose frowned at Philip as he sauntered over to the door. "Don't think that we're not going to finish this conversation later," she told him.

"I wouldn't dream of it," Philip assured her, before giving her a quick, teasing smile, and then heading out with the guard. "I know you will fight me on the matter of your health."

"I was talking about Isra," Rose called after him. She closed the door behind him.

"I wonder what the King wanted," Mary said.

"Well, we are heading to Einish soon," Rose said. "I imagine, from what I've seen of those two, he just wanted to spend more time with him. Maybe they are reviewing over their plans for helping us take care of any Magdust traders we find."

"They are good people," Mary said. "And good brothers."

"Speaking of good brothers," Sophia said, "I wonder where mine has gotten off to. He's supposed to help me load up my tools."

"He's probably already doing that with Theo," Rose said. "Either that, or he's training with him again. We should do more training too, come to think of it, Sophie. It's been a few days since we went over fighting techniques."

"I think it's better we've slowed down some. If I can let Ethan catch up with me, he'll make a good sparring partner. Plus, I can try a few more things I learned from King Derick's blacksmiths. They have some interesting tricks about melting metals and controlling the heat."

Rose felt a small feeling of dismay at Sophia's admission. As much as she had wanted to train Sophia to be a knight, Sophia was more interested in her smithing, as she had always been. As frustrated as it made Rose feel, it was nice Sophia was interested enough that she could help Ethan develop his skills.

One day, Rose thought, they both might need it, especially if she was not able to break her curse.

"How's the sword?" Sophia asked.

"Perfect, as usual." Rose smiled at her, before sheathing the sword in the scabbard at her belt. "Thanks, Sophie."

There was a bright gleam in Sophia's mismatched brown and blue-green eyes. "You know you're always welcome, Rose."

"It'll be ready when we find those Magdust traders. If we leave now, we can arrive at O'Lin before nightfall tomorrow."

"I wish you wouldn't push so much, Rose. You do need to take better care of yourself," Sophia replied. "We love you, you know. All of us."

"You know," Mary said, "it wouldn't hurt us much if we were to leave tomorrow morning, Rose, instead of heading out tonight. You really should rest more."

"It would make the rest of us feel better," Sophia agreed. "Besides, Mary sure likes the mattresses here better than the ones we use on the road."

Rose knew when she was cornered. "Philip is trying to get me to agree with him by using tricks and humor, while you're content to pour on the guilt. Is that it, Sophie?"

"Is it working?"

Rose grimaced. "If it is, I'll never admit to it."

"I thought as much." Sophia laughed. "Here, let me go ahead and have you check the other weapons I brought you. I have your knife here, Rose. And I have Theo and Philip's as well for you to approve."

"Shouldn't they be the ones to approve?"

"They're busy with other stuff, and this is easy. Come on, we'll get some food right after. You're likely hungry, so it's something important you can do, and then you can go eat and feel like you've had a productive morning even though you slept through all of it."

Not all of it, Rose thought. But seeing Sophia's eagerness and feeling the groaning hunger in her own stomach, she conceded to Sophia's direction. "Alright. If you are all so worried about my health, then I will agree we can leave to-morrow morning, rather than tonight. But it's early bedtime for everyone, and there will be no exceptions."

Despite her reluctance to delay their departure, Rose felt better about her decision when Sophia and Mary both cheered.

ONCE UPON A PRINCESS

7

As the morning dawned, Theo congratulated himself on having avoided Rose successfully since the embarrassing incident down in the hot springs. He told himself to take comfort in the time he'd had to reflect on what he would say to her, and how she would react, because there was no avoiding her on this day.

Theo prayed for extra mercy that morning.

He heard a knock at the door to his and answered it, fearing the devil was already going to give him grief.

When he saw Roderick's rust-colored beard and large girth in the doorway, he almost sank to his knees in gratitude.

"Sir," Roderick greeted. "Captain Locke and Lannister are getting the horses ready now. We will be ready to depart as soon as everyone is ready."

"Excellent," Theo said. "That's good news."

"Good news for the Princess," Roderick said. "But I for one will miss the comforts of the castle. Crystal Lake is a beautiful place."

"Your accommodations were to your liking?"

"Oh, yes," Roderick nodded. "It was much easier to slip out to the town at night than I thought it would be."

"Did you and the others learn anything interesting about what's going on in the woods?" Theo asked. "I know King Derick has been looking into it, but he has a lot of other concerns."

"He has quite a few loyal men to delegate the task to," Roderick said. "I talked with many of them while I was in town."

"What about the city residents? I know there are places you can get into that he couldn't. At least, not without a good disguise."

"True enough. The King does have some subjects who are more than reluctant to face the unification of Einish and Crystal Lake. He will likely have to deal with later." Roderick chuckled. "But besides that, there's not much I did find out about the trouble between the countries at their borders. All I have been able to discover for sure is that it is connected with the Magdust trade."

"That's what Philip told me and Rose," Theo said.

"I've heard some other rumors, but I could not verify them. I have to admit I'm a little hesitant to share them with you."

"What? Why?"

"There are rumors that Magdalina herself has been spotted in the forest between Einish and Rhone, close to where Crystal Lake also borders the two."

"We will be going right through that area," Theo said. "At least, according to Ethan, that is."

"Yes. I don't want you or the Princess to get your hopes up."

"What about Everon?" Theo asked, thinking of the large, brutish fairy who had killed his parents. Despite his upbringing, Theo felt his blood hum with vengeful anticipation.

"He has not been spotted, just Magdalina," Roderick said. "Again, that was just a rumor, and I have no solid consensus on it."

Theo's optimism plummeted. "Oh."

"I'm curious," Roderick mused, "how she would have been able to come into this place at all, though."

"What do you mean?" Theo asked.

"From what the people I talked to told me, the pixies who reside in Crystal Lake have no love of fairies, that's for sure, but they have had a peaceful coexistence for years."

"I remember Mary saying something about the pixies," Theo said. "She said they were friendly."

"Not a lot of them, really. I was able to learn more about them when I was in town. Pixies have, in the past, used their own spells and power to keep fairies, even those such as Magdalina, from moving onto their territory. So it is interesting that the Magdust trade has expanded to the Wandering Caverns."

"What do you think it means? Based on what you've heard?"

"As I see it, there are only a few things it could be." Roderick sighed. "It's possible the pixies are working with the traders, or they have been ambushed by the traders themselves."

Theo frowned. "But how would the traders overpower them?"

"Magic has rules, remember?" Roderick stroked his beard thoughtfully. "Pixies have their own rules, different from the fairies; it's part of the reason they don't live together very often. If a human was able to control a pixie, it would be easy for them to attack the fairies and also move in on the pixies' territory. It also makes it easier to make Magdust when you already have magic, from what I heard down by the prison."

"I've never thought about what it takes to make Magdust," Theo admitted. "I just knew the fairies are killed for their power. I know there are ways to kill fairies, but butchering them for their power is a whole different thing. I didn't think about that before."

Roderick snorted. "Well, you wouldn't, would you? The idea of Magdust is already unpleasant enough."

"The Magdust trade goes back many years," Roderick said. "I've listened to a lot of people's stories, and most of them agree that the fairies have become endangered because of Rhone's first leader. He was the one, they tell me, that first used it to gain power."

"That's true. Titania, Queen Lucia's daughter, told us as much when the rest of us were looking for her," Theo said. "She said Benedict used the Magdust to gain power over Lucia. Once she was out of the way, he was able to establish himself as the ruler of Rhone, rather than just a knight."

"Yes, but he was far from the only person who knew how to make the Magdust," Roderick said. "So other people knew about it and how to make it."

Theo thought of his mother, whose face seemed blurry in his memory after more than decade without her. He thought of his father, too, who was more knight than father in his memory. "I can agree to that," he said.

Roderick sighed. "It can be profitable. Even if you are not a king, you could live like one if you were able to sell enough."

"I think that's why my father was in it," Theo admitted quietly.

He thought back to the unpleasant conversation he'd had with his older brother the last time he had been in Rhone. Thad had told him the truth of what he'd found from their Uncle Thom, who had also been killed by Everon and his cronies.

Of all the people from his past, it was his uncle that remained completely real against the passage of time. The breadth of his shoulders, the warmth of his laugh, the blood splattered on his beard and hands and back as he tried to get

Theo and Thad out of their home the night his parents died. All of Uncle Thom still seemed very vivid in comparison to the memories of his parents.

They walked down the hall some, when Theo stopped by the tapestry of Queen Lucia. The wall drapery, with all its advanced weaving and skill, made him wonder. He reached out and grabbed Roderick's arm. "Do you know someone managed to weave the Magdust into fabric?"

"I've heard some tales. Magdust was used by some sorcerers for any number of things." Roderick looked up at the tapestry alongside Theo. "Why? Do you think this one has some in it?"

"It looks a lot like one my mother had hanging in our house," Theo said. "I'd love to know if it does."

"How did you destroy it?"

"My uncle burned it," Theo said.

"Makes sense," Roderick said with a nod.

"What do you mean?" Theo asked. "Why would that work?"

"Fairies are very, very cautious around fire," Roderick said. "They are creatures of creation, you know. Mary is proof of that, isn't she? You can see that they have no trouble creating something new, or even making something different, but they do not use the power to destroy. When they need light, they usually collect sunlight or even moonlight."

"That's true." Theo nodded. It would explain why fairy magic would not work around dragons and their blood.

"Fire, on the other hand, is a natural destroyer." Roderick shrugged. "But I'm not sure King Derick would be happy if you burned up his tapestry and there was nothing wrong with it."

Theo did not like to think about it, but he had an idea. "Maybe Rose can use her sword to find out if there's Magdust in it somehow."

"No harm in trying," Roderick agreed. "We'd likely get better results than trying to burn it, if nothing else."

"There might be no harm in trying," Theo said, "but I'm hoping there is no harm in asking. I wouldn't want to inconvenience Rose."

"She does have a temper," Roderick agreed. "I properly pity anyone who has the gall to make her upset."

"Me, too," Theo muttered. "Me, too."

Rose already had a list of reasons to argue with Theo over something, so she was even more unhappy when she opened her door in the morning and there was Roderick, who Theo had sent to her room in order to summon her to his side.

"I'm in charge," Rose reminded Roderick. "Theo doesn't have the right to order me to come see him."

"It was a poor choice of words on my part, My Lady."

Rose scoffed. "Rose, please. You know I hate formality between friends."

"We are friends then?"

"I guess so," Rose told him, giving him one of her smiles. She appreciated that his cheeks dulled with a pleasing flush; Roderick was smart enough to know that her trust was hard won.

Now, it is time to remind Theo of that as well.

But despite her anger, Rose forced herself to act normally when she saw him. "What did you want, Theo, that was so important that you ordered me away from breakfast?"

ONCE UPON A PRINCESS

"You haven't eaten yet," Theo told her easily enough. "I know you well, Rose. You pack your breakfast to go and eat it while we're on the road."

"For your information, I was going to go to the dining hall before you sent for me."

"But not to eat. Just to get food. It's still different."

She glared at him, no doubt angry because he was right. "Well, now that you've ruined my appetite, what do you need me for?"

Theo nodded toward the tapestry. "I wanted to see if there was any Magdust in this design," he said.

"Why would you think it does?" Rose scowled. She glanced up at the tapestry once more, where Queen Lucia's gaze was just as imposing as it had been the day before.

"My mother had one that carried Magdust," Theo told her quietly. "It was very similar to this one."

Rose raised her eyebrows at that. She sighed, and some part of her had to admit she could not keeping looking for a fight to pick with him.

They had work to do, both of them, and bickering every step of the way there was not going to help. And Theo did not talk much about his parents or his past before he came to Rhone's capital. If he thought this was important, she had a duty to comply.

"What do you think we can do?" Rose asked. "I talked with Juliette about this tapestry yesterday. She said it was a gift from one of the Einish court ambassadors."

"I was thinking your sword might be able to do something," Theo said. "Remember when you were jousting with Marsor on Maltia? You were able to shatter his sword and find the stash of Magdust the hilt had."

Rose pulled out her sword. "I'd hate to cut this," she said. "I mean, if it's just a normal tapestry."

"Well, the fairy magic should still respond to it, right?" Roderick asked. "Just use your sword to touch it gently."

Feeling silly, Rose pressed the tip of her sword against the tapestry.

For a moment, nothing happened. All of them seemed to be holding their breaths, waiting for something to happen.

Then, slowly, a small pink-and-green glow emitted from the point where the sword and the fabric came together.

"I was right." Theo's expression was grim and glad at the same time. "There is Magdust in it."

"We'd better tell the King," Rose said. She pulled her sword away from the tapestry. Immediately, the shimmering cloud of dust disappeared back into the folds of the fabric. "He needs to get rid of this, before he's accused of helping the Magdust trade flourish."

"I'll go and get him," Roderick offered. "You two can stay here." He was already sprinting down the hallway when Rose started to object.

"No, that's alright—" Rose tried to stop him, wanting to insist that she would go and get the King, that it would be her great pleasure, that she should be the one to break the bad news. But it was too late.

She was forced to be alone with Theo.

I hate this. This situation would have never bothered me before.

"So, did you get enough sleep last night?" Theo asked. His tone, inquiring and calm, was the same as it had always been, as he asked her the question he must have asked her a million times or more.

ONCE UPON A PRINCESS

It irritated Rose to no end. "Yes," she replied, determined to show him that two could play the normal game. "How about you? How is your back?"

"It is getting better."

His tone was the same, Rose noticed, but he wasn't looking at her.

"You said your mother had one of these?" Rose asked, gesturing to the tapestry.

"She said that my father won it at a tournament," Theo said. "She had a gift for weaving herself though. I remember she used to spent a lot of time at her spinning wheel, before the King outlawed and destroyed them."

Rose only nodded. "Juliette told me that there was a famous weaver who made these and sold them at tournaments, so it fits."

"Is the weaver still alive, do you think?" Theo asked. "We might be able to find out more about it from her."

"Well, Juliette said she died. But she had children. And there's always the possibility she had an apprentice or her teacher could still be alive. Tradesmen and artisans of all kinds would have apprentices. Even Sophie gets excited when we're at a place where she can learn about a new tool or technique." Rose sighed. "I'm actually worried she might not want to be a knight at all, considering her interest still lies in blacksmithing."

"She's still a good fighter. And a good squire. Not all squires make it to knighthood," Theo reminded her gently. "Even though I know you wanted her to succeed as a lady knight."

"It's fine," Rose said, waving the issue aside. "I guess we need to be more concerned with the weaver right now than

Sophia's trade. Juliette said she got this from someone at the Einish court. We can ask around when we get there."

"Maybe Isra will be able to tell us something, too."

Rose nodded. "Maybe. She hasn't sent any letters back lately."

"She knows we're close."

"True." Rose glanced out the nearby window, looking up at the clouds. "But I miss Virtue."

Her gyrfalcon, with his large wings and his soulful eyes, acted as a messenger between her worlds. She decided to herself that when she saw him again, she would take a few hours and go hawking with him.

"Rose."

She flinched; the past few moments had been nice, almost normal. Hearing Theo say her name ruined it.

"What?" she bit back.

"I talked with Roderick some," he said. "He and the others were able to find some information for us."

"Oh?" Rose lost her defensiveness immediately. "Anything interesting?"

"There are rumors—just rumors—that Magdalina has been spotted in the Einish forest."

Rose's hand tightened around her sword hilt. "That means that we might ... "

"We might get a chance to fight her," Theo concluded.

"I'm ready." "I'm more than willing to engage Magdalina in battle. She might have caught me by surprised at my birthday party this past year, but she's no match for me with a sword."

"Especially one with dragon's blood," Theo agreed. "She won't be able to stand up to that."

Rose nodded. "I could finally be free," she whispered.

"That's right." Theo gave her a grin, meeting her eyes for the first time. "And then you'll be able to sing again."

Rose flushed.

"You never did sing for me," Theo reminded her. "You still have to do that."

Rose scowled. *Just when I thought things were starting to go alright,* she thought bitterly. She crossed her arms, folding her sword underneath her arm. "Can you just forget about that? I mean, after yesterday's incident, we should be even."

Pure hatred, mostly for herself, throbbed through her, drowning her in self-inflicted rage. She saw the change in Theo's expression immediately, and she knew he was not happy with her remark, either.

"Fine," he said. "We'll call it even."

"Good," Rose snapped back. "And I don't want to talk about it anymore."

"Fine."

"*Fine.*"

"There's no need for you to be a brat about it," Theo told her. "Your behavior is hardly mature."

Rose stuck her tongue out at him.

Before Theo could reply, Roderick and Derick came into sight. Juliette was not far behind the two of them.

Rose greeted her with a smile, but it was not enough to ease the worry she saw on Juliette's expression.

"Rose," Derick said. "Good morning. Starting the day's adventures early, are you?"

"Apparently," Rose said, trying to match the chipper tone of the King's, even though her mood was far from cheerful, and the news she had for them even less so.

When Rose placed the tip of her sword back against the tapestry, Juliette gasped in horror.

"What do we do?" Derick asked.

"Burn it," Theo said. "I know from experience it's the easiest way of getting rid of it."

"What about the baby?" Juliette asked. "Will the baby be alright?"

"What about it?" Rose looked over at her. Juliette reached out and took Derick's hand for support.

"If we get rid of the tapestry, it wouldn't hurt the baby, will it?" Juliette looked distressed. "Ambassador Rolez told me that it was supposed to bring good luck for babies and their health. He said it was supposed to protect our children."

"That's likely just superstition," Rose said, watching as Juliette put her arms protectively over her tummy again. Rose struggled to feel sympathy for Juliette, but she was unable to muster much. The Queen's reaction seemed too much like an overreaction. Wasn't Juliette the one, after all, who had told her before she didn't believe the tapestry was actually magic? Why would she worry that getting rid of it would somehow harm her child?

Rose knew she was not the one to handle this anymore. She immediately looked to Theo. He was better with this sort of thing, she thought. "Theo?"

Theo immediately jumped forward and began comforting Juliette, while Roderick and Derick began to take the tapestry down from the wall.

It wasn't long before Theo sent Juliette down to the chapel, along with Derick to support her, and the tapestry was burning in a nearby fireplace.

Rose watched it burn, her eyes following the ballooning puffs of pink and green shimmers. "I guess the Magdust trade is more complicated than just transporting it in its powder form."

Theo stoked the fire with a poker. "If it makes you feel better," he said, "it has been going on for decades now. It won't be an easy fix."

"If it's been going on for decades, why hasn't Rhone been able to do much about it?" Rose asked. "Isn't that why Magdalina and her forces are so angry with the people of Rhone?"

"Wars like this are cyclical," Theo replied. "They come and go, almost like the tides. Where there is the opportunity to engage in profitable activity, there are people who indulge it in. And then there are people who educate themselves and others on how to stay away from it. It is a war on the individual that has consequences for the whole community."

"Do you think once Magdalina is no longer a concern, we will still face this problem?" Rose asked.

"There will be years of repair that we will need to do with the fairyfolk who are upset with us," Theo said. "Magdalina is only one symptom of a larger problem."

Rose smiled sadly. "So, yes then?"

He nodded.

She sighed. "It seems too big of a problem."

"Not when we can face it together, Rosary," Theo said. "And *that* is something you don't have to worry about."

He stuffed the poker back in its place and stood up. Rose was about to thank him for his kindness when he added, "Even if I did happen to see you soaking wet, half-clothed in your undergarments."

"What's that about seeing Rose in her undergarments?" Philip asked as he came into the room.

Rose scowled at Theo. "You're the worst," she hissed, angry at him all over again. If he was getting back at her for her earlier remarks, he could not have done a better job, she thought bitterly.

Philip looked surprised. "So something actually happened? What's the story?" he asked. "Tell me."

"No," Rose snapped. "It's none of your concern."

"Come on, Rose—"

"No." She huffed and then stormed toward the door. "Now that the Magdust has been taken care of, let's go say our final goodbyes to your brother, Philip. If we want to get to Einish sooner rather than later, we better get going."

She didn't wait around for their reactions; she felt their lingering stares as she headed out of the room and down the hall.

Rose briefly glanced back at the blank wall, where Queen Lucia's tapestry had hung only moments before. The brocade of the Queen's portrait was gone, but she still felt the shadow of Lucia's soft and condemning judgment as she made her way out of the palace.

8

"So," Philip goaded as he galloped up next to her, "Tell me about what happened."

"No." Rose gripped her horse's bridle in her hands, glad to be riding again, even if it was as much a pain on her bottom as walking was on her feet. She prepared herself for the worst; they had already been on the road for a full day, and Philip had tried several different times to get her to explain Theo's remarks about seeing her in her undergarments.

"Do you want me to get the details out of him?" Philip asked.

"No!" Rose glared at him. "Stop. I'm not talking about it, he's not going to talk about it, and you need to stop worrying about it."

"You *do* want to talk about it, though," Philip said with a teasing laugh. "I can tell by the look on your face."

"What look?"

"The one that says you have something on your mind, and you're more than cross about it. Come on, Rose, tell me. You might feel better. After all, I'm your babysitter, remember?"

"Is that actually the word Isra used?" Rose shook the sweat out of her eyes, taking the moment to glance over their caravan.

"Well, it was the one you used."

Mary was riding with Sophia and Ethan, jumping from one horse to another as they talked about the history of the Magdust trade. Theo was right behind them, probably lost in some prayer or some other deep kind of thoughts. The guards, led by Captain Locke, were at the rear, with Roderick's ruddy beard served as a marker, one Rose could easily

71

use to see the end of her traveling company. Beside her, Philip took the lead in guiding them to his home.

Rose turned back to Philip. "Did she use it too?"

"No," he said. "But Isra did make me promise to see to your care. This would include discussing what troubles you."

Rose rolled her eyes. Her sister, not even two years younger than her, had an insurmountable amount of charm. It was not hard for Rose to see that Philip had fallen into Isra's close counsel. If the situation was any different, and if Philip were more ruthless, Rose knew she might have suspected Philip of using Isra to gain her trust.

Maybe he would even use my sister to secure an offer of marriage from me, Rose thought, momentarily cynical.

But she doubted that he would do that. He had been her friend, and that was all. She respected him and she admired him, but that was all. Philip was her friend.

"I'd rather talk about the Magdust trade here in the Einish forest," Rose finally told him. "Did Derick give you any new information since he discussed it with us that night at dinner?"

"No," Philip said. "In all fairness, he was more concerned with consoling Juliette after this morning to give me any last minute details."

"I don't understand her reaction to burning the tapestry," Rose admitted.

"I know that there are some concerns over destroying artifacts that are embedded with magic. Like you said, it is more superstition than truth. But where children are concerned, including the future ruler of Einish and Crystal Lake, mothers worry about their children quite desperately."

"But Juliette had told me before that she didn't think the tapestry was magic, as some people have maintained."

"I don't see her reactions as that unusual. People are more likely to believe in bad luck than good luck." Philip straightened in his saddle, taking them down the left side of a split trail.

Rose shrugged. "I guess so. I'm sure my mother would agree with you."

Philip nodded and said nothing. They both knew that Rose's mother had faced the terrifying reality of Rose's curse.

Rose had to wonder if Philip pitied her, because his hazel eyes seemed sad when he looked back at her.

Maybe that is why he wants to know so much about what happened with Theo, Rose thought. He wanted to distract her with one set of problems while they faced another.

Before she could tell Philip not to waste his time worrying about her, Mary appeared at her side.

"We're about to go through the Crystal Lake's Wandering Caverns," she said. "This is where a lot of the trade activity has been rumored to take place."

"Stay with me," Rose told her. "I don't want anything happening to you. I can protect you better with Queen Lucia's sword if something goes wrong."

Mary nodded. "Thank you, Rose," she said, as she climbed into the hood of Rose's cloak. "I'm not surprised that this is the area where a lot trouble has been brewing. The pixies who lived here have retracted their protective spells."

"Pixies live here?" Rose asked.

"Pixies are able to withstand more extreme environments," Mary explained. "They are not as afraid of fire and volcanic activity as fairies are. They have made the caverns their home for many centuries."

"I didn't know you were afraid of volcanoes."

73

"Not exactly. Iron and other minerals can harm us just as badly as more powerful magic or if we are injured enough by other weapons," Mary said. "It occurs naturally in volcanoes, which is why you are more likely to find fairies in the woods or by the sea. There are some fairies that have the power to stand up to the elements, but the majority of us cannot."

"Good to know," Rose whispered. "In the meantime, I'll keep you safe as we go the caverns."

"We likely won't have to worry," Mary said, even though she shivered. "But it's best not to tempt fate."

"That's true."

"The path leads through the caverns," Philip said. "We'll need to stick together while we're in there."

"There are still some enchantments in place from pixies," Mary warned. "So we need to watch out for them as much as we need to watch out for Magdust traders."

"Pixie magic, huh?" Philip grinned. "I'd forgotten about that. But then, this is the Wandering Caverns, isn't it?"

"What are you worried about?" Rose asked.

Mary tugged on her dress, nervous and distressed. "This place is one of the places where the pixies made the tunnels shift as you walk through them," she said. "It might be hard to navigate. I can't read pixie magic the way I can fairy mag-ic."

Ethan came up beside Rose. "Are we really going to go in there?"

"Yes, Ethan," Philip answered. "Yes, we'll need to go into the caves. It's only for a little while."

"I don't have anything on the map for it," Ethan said, brandishing one of the many scrolls he carried in his pack.

"The forest has a trail," Philip replied. "The map just doesn't show that the main path leads through a cave. We're still going in the right direction."

"If it's enchanted I don't like the idea of going in," Ethan said. "Especially without a solid map of the place and rumors of the illegal traders."

"We'll just have to be careful about it," Rose said. She halted her mare and dismounted. "We've had similar situations before."

"Yeah, which is why I'm nervous about it," Ethan told her.

Rose pretended she didn't hear his remark. "Let's go ahead and partner up as we go into the cave. I'll lead."

"But what if you don't know which way to go?" Philip asked. "I should lead on this one, Rose."

"You can stay behind me," Rose told him. "And anyway, you just said that the main trail just went through the cavern. How hard could it be to follow the map while we're in the cave?"

Mary chimed in. "If Rose leads," she said, "I'll be able to light the way for everyone better. And Philip can be on the lookout for the traders, since he is more familiar with the cave."

"I'm not familiar with the cave. I'm only familiar with the path on the map," Philip insisted, but he was largely ignored as Rose and Ethan studied the map together.

"What's wrong?" Theo asked, coming up beside them.

"Nothing," Rose told him. "We're checking the map."

"We need to get in pairs," Ethan said. "Mary and Rose can go in front, since that will help with lighting. And Mary can sense some magic, so it might be good to have her out in front."

Philip looked over at Theo. "We can follow them," he said. "You take one side, I'll take the other, and we'll be able to anticipate any trouble for Rose or for Ethan and Sophia."

"Why do I have to be paired up with Ethan?" Sophia asked. She had already dismounted from her horse, and she was tapping her foot impatiently.

"Just do it," Rose said. "If Ronan were here, I would protect him."

"Easy for you to say since he's not," Sophia accused, but she took her place beside Ethan without further protest.

"The guards will be able to protect the rear," Rose said. "Swords out and ready, but be sure before you strike. The pixies who might be in here have never been a threat to Rhone."

Rose was glad to see there were no objections as they headed in.

Once she was in the cave, Rose couldn't help slowing her steps. She found her eyes lingering on some of the crystalline rocks; they were colored and bright, cheery enough to dispel any forethought of danger.

"This place is beautiful," she whispered to Mary.

"The pixies are a studious lot," Mary said. "They value beauty above nature. I wouldn't be surprised to find several of these crystals have been curated specifically for their magic."

"The crystals hold magic in them?" Rose asked.

"Not all of them. But some of them, I'm sure. These are likely fake, to distract any marauders from finding the real treasure."

"Distraction," Rose murmured thoughtfully.

"Yes," Mary agreed.

They walked slowly through the cave. Time passed by at an unknowing pace, as they made their way deeper into the heart of the cave.

Eventually, Rose started to notice the hard ground beneath her boots. She blinked and realized she had to have been walking for at least an hour.

Philip further interrupted the spell that had fallen on them when he announced, "We're almost halfway through the cave."

Rose glanced back. "Everyone doing okay?"

A small round of murmurs, replying in the affirmative with their words and in the negative with their tone, answered her query. The roof of the cave began to curl back, opening up into a larger room, where light poked through the roof and fell on the shimmering crystal-lined walls. They glowed with a brilliant light. Rose faltered as she watched the twinkling colors blink at her. She called back to her crew. "We can take a break up here for a little while."

"That's a relief," Mary murmured, as she settled onto Rose's mare.

Rose giggled. "You seem rather comfy," she said.

"It does not mean I wouldn't like a break."

The rest of her friends and traveling companions agreed with more cheerfulness. The thought of water, food, and sitting down stopped several of their echoed grumblings.

Rose was glancing up at the ceiling as it opened up into an even larger cavern when she heard Philip call, "Watch out, Rose!"

"What? What is it?"

He never had to answer her. Rose saw a pair of big, burly shadows detach from the side of the cave and step out in front of her. "Traders!" Rose brandished her sword.

A small band appeared behind the men, their own weapons held aloft and ready to strike.

Time to fight! Rose stepped forward.

Everything seemed to happen at once. The band of traders rushed at them, but Rose ducked and rolled, sending some of them falling fast. Theo and Philip teamed up to take down several of the men surrounding Rose, while Sophia, Ethan, and the rest of the guards alternatively protected the supplies and attacked the traders who came too close to their camp.

Rose heard her horse jitter nervously, and she hurried to calm her. Before she could tighten her grip on her bridle, the horse reared and headed off, further into the cave, while Mary screamed in fear.

"Mary!" Rose cried, watching as her fairy clung to the horse's mane.

"Go get her, Rose," Theo yelled, charging toward the men. He pushed Rose forward, sending her running. "We can cover for you."

"But—"

"Just go, Rose," Philip called out. He blocked another opponent, fighting with a new bandit who appeared behind them.

Rose sighed as her horse neighed again, the terror in the beast's cry echoing back into the atrium. "I'll be back as soon as I can!" Rose turned and headed after her horse.

It didn't take her long to catch up with the wayward horse; she caught up with them to find Mary had cast a spell on the horse, rendering the horse motionless.

"Mary!" Rose called. "I'm glad you're safe."

"I forgot I can do magic," Mary admitted sheepishly. "I know, I know. But I was taken off guard when she started running."

Rose gave her a nervous laugh. "I understand. I'm just glad you're okay. You can unfreeze her now."

As the mare became animated once more, Rose's hands tightened around the reins. The horse skittered around fretfully, still in mid-motion. Rose fought to keep her footing, while Mary continued to cling onto the horse tightly.

As Rose managed to stop her frightened mare, she noticed the fighting behind her had gone quiet.

Rose turned around and saw she was suddenly alone with Mary and her horse. She ran back in the direction she had come, only to find the blackened walls of the cavern wall had closed in on her.

"Rose," Mary said. "We must have stepped into a trap." She jumped from the mare's back into the hood of Rose's cloak.

"We need to step out of it then," Rose said, circling the small, circular cave. "Stay down in case this was a trap set by the Magdust traders."

A familiar voice spoke out of the shadows. "I wouldn't worry about the Magdust traders. Your friends are fighting them as we speak. They're winning, too, which is really no surprise. Not after the Eastern Warlords you battled two years ago."

Rose gasped, hurriedly raising her sword into a fighting position as Magdalina's bright face appeared out of the darkness.

Rose's hands held fast to her hilt, and she was determined to fight the ruler of the fairies who had cursed her.

This is it! I can be free, if I can defeat her.

"What are you doing here, Magdalina?" Rose asked. "Have you come to punish the traders?"

"Why, no," Magdalina said. "The fairyfolk have largely rejected me as a member of their community, even though I am their leader. It doesn't actually bother me if they are killed. But I thought that it would be a good reason to have you come this way."

Rose faltered only slightly. "Why did you want us to come here, if not to punish the traders?"

"Well, your friends are taking care of them for me now," Magdalina said. "Just take a look, if you want."

A white hand wafted gracefully out of the darkness, and pointed to the wall to Rose's side. Rose glanced over to see the rock turn transparent. She watched as several bandits attacked her friends. She could hear their shouts and the clash of their swords against the enemy's blades.

She could only allow it a second of her time before she turned her full attention back to Magdalina. To her credit, Magdalina had not moved, so far as Rose could see. Her eyes adjusted to the dark, and she thought she could make out the edges of Magdalina's black robes and the high atora on her head. Her magical staff appeared in her hands as she began to walk toward Rose.

Rose saw the small gleam of her sword's ruby. The dragon's blood was reacting to Magdalina's presence.

Rose took a strong step forward, her sword ready to strike. She let it swipe down hard, but the second before it touched her, Magdalina disappeared.

"Come out and fight," Rose called. "You coward!"

"I hardly call being smart enough to avoid death being a coward."

"You dodge battles and place curses on innocent children," Rose scoffed. "I'd say that's pretty cowardly. You punished me when I was just a baby. I didn't do anything to you."

"I know."

Rose gritted her teeth together. "How is that not being a coward?"

"I told you before, I was punishing your father," Magdalina said.

"Why?" Rose blurted out, as she dropped her sword ever so slightly. She hoped Magdalina would see it as exhaustion. Beside her, she could still see through the rock wall, where Philip, Theo, and the guards were leading the attack against a large band of men.

She knew she had to defeat Magdalina, and the quicker she was able to take care of her, the sooner she could join her friends.

"Even if you cursed me to punish my father, you know I have a right to fight you for what you've done."

"I agree. Still, I'd rather not die," Magdalina said. "I know you have acquired the dragon's blood. No easy feat, and you are so young and naïve besides. You are a formidable opponent. But I don't want to fight you."

"Then remove the curse from me!" Rose cried, lunging out with her sword once more, searching for any target to strike. Her sword scrapped into the other side of the cave.

Magdalina appeared behind her. "I might not want to fight you, but I have something else I wish to discuss with you. I have given this a great deal of thought," she said. "So much so that I have traveled a great distance to get here. I have decided to offer you a deal."

Rose stopped moving, shocked. Her grip on her sword went limp, and immediately she felt Mary's small hands grabbing onto her cloak's collar, as if to remind her to keep her guard strong.

Rose adjusted her stance and tightened her grip. "What kind of deal?"

Magdalina's red lips parted as she smiled. "Do you want to know what your father did to me, that I placed such a curse on you?"

"I thought we were making a deal," Rose huffed.

"We are. I want to make the same deal with you that I made with your father."

Rose had a hard time keeping her fighting stance strong. "What was the deal?" she finally asked, standing up straight once more. She decided that she still had plenty of time to protect herself from a possible attack. .

She kept her fingers tight against the hilt of her sword as she asked once more, "What was the deal?"

"You know enough about Rhone's history to know that my mother was supposed to be the nation's first queen," Magdalina said. "When Benedict betrayed her and sealed her away, he eventually married another, a lady who was already a queen in her own land, as small as it was. Together, their rule made up the present-day borders of the kingdom."

"So what?" Rose asked.

"So," Magdalina said, "I could have been queen myself, once. I am Lucia's daughter, after all."

Rose frowned. She doubted that would have worked, considering Benedict had been the first king. He would have wanted his own offspring to rule, not Lucia's other children.

"Since then, the fairyfolk have harbored a great deal of mistrust of the crown. Occasionally, they would try to work together. Your little friend there is proof that some within the fairy community have managed to ingratiate themselves to the monarchy."

Rose raised her sword, protecting Mary from Magdalina's gaze.

"I am already going to do what I can to get rid of the Mag-dust trade, if that was the deal," Rose said.

The instant she heard herself say the words, she knew that was not the deal Magdalina was talking about. Magdalina had just admitted moments before that she didn't care if the fair-ies were killed. They had rejected her, and only served her out of fear of her power or out of hatred for Rhone's rulers.

"They could have had their own ruler on the throne," Mag-dalina said. "So when your father came to me, I promised to give him what he wanted, in exchange for the promise that his firstborn would marry a fairy of my choice."

"What did my father want?" Rose asked, not certain she wanted to hear.

"A child. What else?" Magdalina laughed. "He desperately wanted children. He is getting old, haven't you noticed? He was married to Leea for many years before they had you and your half-siblings."

"The King told me that he'd received word from a prophet of the church that I was going to be born and I would save the crown," Rose said, feeling foolish for even saying it.

Magdalina waved her arm dismissively. "So?" she said. "If that's true, it still does not make a difference. I don't care if you save the crown. In fact, I hope you do."

She took another step toward Rose. "Here is my deal: I want you to marry my son, and make him King of Rhone."

"What?" Rose tasted the bile at the thought. "Never. That's a terrible deal. And it's annoying. Why are so many people so concerned about me getting married? Haven't I proven that I'm more than some marriage prize?"

"You should consider it an honor," Magdalina said. "Men might be seen as the great conquerors of the world, but look at all the destruction they leave in their wake. Men destroy things, men shape things. But they cannot create new life. Only a woman has the power to create life, to create a new path for an old world to walk."

Rose felt her mouth drop open, unsure of her complete reaction. Magdalina had a point. "It still seems unfair."

"Oh, do stop worrying so much about what is unfair with this world," Magdalina muttered. "Life isn't fair, Princess, and you and I are prime examples. But the fact remains, if you want me to remove the curse I placed on you, I will, but only if you agree to marry my son, Everon, and make him the next ruler of Rhone. Whole civilizations depend on their women, and you have the chance to end the decades of distrust between my family and my subjects."

Pure rage ate at Rose's insides.

"So there you have it. All you have to do is marry my son, and I will free you from my curse, even at the cost of my own life."

Rose glanced down as Magdalina held up her wrist. She said before she had put a blood seal on the spell, Rose recalled.

Rose turned her attention back to her sword.

As if she knew what Rose was thinking, Magdalina laughed. "Please. You won't kill me. All I have to do is avoid you."

"You can't avoid me forever!" Rose yelled back.

"I don't have to avoid you forever," Magdalina said. "I only have to wait until your eighteenth birthday. It's less than a year away now, isn't it? How much longer do I have to wait? Only about five months, right?"

Rose said nothing at her taunting; she only took another step forward, securing the hilt of her sword in both hands.

"Maybe as you get closer to the date, you'll reconsider my offer. I'll give you until then for you to decide. That seems fair, doesn't it? I should give you everything up until the moment when you have to choose between marriage to my son and fateful sleep." Magdalina's voice was smooth with confidence and power. Her elegance made Rose feel even more helpless when it came to her fate.

"I'll never succumb to the curse," Rose declared. "I'll never choose either. Never!"

"We will see," Magdalina replied, before she disappeared in a ball of greenish flames. A flurry of stormy wind blew out from the center of her power, pushing Rose back up against her horse.

They were once more alone; Rose could hear her friends fighting in the distance once more.

"Rose," Mary gasped. "Are you alright?"

Rose felt her body shake, as she struggled to maintain her posture. Her legs felt weak. "I'm fine," she lied, trying to steady herself.

"I'm here for you," Mary whispered.

"I wish it were so easy," Rose said, her voice cracking. She put a hand to her throat, forcing herself not to cry, no matter how angry or sad she was.

Mary's tiny caress of her hair made her feel better as she slumped against the floor. "How do we get out of here?" Rose asked. "We have to go and help the others."

"I can try a spell," Mary offered. "I wasn't able to work my magic while I was so close to Magdalina. She is much more powerful than I am."

"I was hoping so much, that I would be able to defeat her."

"I know." Mary wrapped her arms around Rose's wrist. "She has always been a formidable opponent. We can learn from this."

"I already have," Rose assured her. "Dragon's blood won't be enough to kill her. I'll need help fighting her, too."

Mary only nodded.

A few moments passed, as Rose rested and tried to regain her focus. She eventually stood up and went back to her horse.

"Rose?" Mary whispered.

"What is it?"

"What do you think of her deal?" Mary asked. "Do you think you will accept it?"

"I might be cursed to sleep forever after I turn eighteen," Rose said, "but it would still be better than being married to Magdalina's son. Theo wants his own revenge against Everon, too, don't forget."

"You said you'd never choose to let your curse be fulfilled," Mary pointed out.

"And I never will," Rose said. "I'm going to defeat her, no matter what, Mary. I have to."

Mary patted her shoulder reassuringly. "Maybe her deal is still something we can work with."

Rose shook her head. "I'm not even going to consider it," she said. "I don't want you to tell anyone what she told me."

"But, Rose, we might—"

"No." Rose shook her head. "No, Mary. Do not tell anyone about this. Especially Theo. Do you hear me?"

"But it's your life."

"And it would be my life that would be ruined," Rose argued. She sighed. "You know what my greatest fear was,

Mary? The one I confronted when I battled the dragon for his blood?"

Mary was silent.

"I want a family. My own family, with my own husband and my own children," Rose said. "Children, who know they are loved and treasured. I want to rule Rhone one day and I will never forgive myself if I cannot free myself from my curse. The idea that I will never be loved, the idea that no one will be able to marry me and start a family with me—it's too much to bear. It's too hard to even admit to myself!"

"But Rose...."

"The very idea that I would marry a fairy like Everon, who is little more than Magdalina's glorified bodyguard or her main stooge, is not only sickening, it is unforgivably vile." Rose shook her head. "I guess at least, if my curse is fulfilled, Isra will be able to inherit the throne."

Another realization struck her, and left her feeling dazed. *Isra ... my half-sister, from what Magdalina just told me.*

"Mary, what did Magdalina mean when she said that Isra and Ronan were my half-siblings?" Rose asked. "They will still be able to inherit the throne, won't they?"

Mary shook her head. "I don't know, Rose. I don't know."

"Was she telling the truth?"

"I don't know," Mary insisted. "That's something we will have to ask your mother when we get back to Rhone."

"Well, let's round up these Magdust traders," Rose said, "and then get back on the road. If our answers are in Rhone, I want to get there as quickly as I can."

9

"How are you doing?" Philip asked Theo, giving him a grin as he lowered his sword, finishing off his adversaries. "I've taken care of these three."

Theo watched as Philip lunged his sword forward, just barely missing the large man who had stepped out and blocked his path moments earlier. "Good shot," he said, as he clashed with another trader.

Theo shuffled low and managed to elbow his opponent in the gut, sending him to the ground, knocked out. "I've got two of them knocked out now," Theo replied.

"Where's the leader?"

"Ethan and Sophia are working on him." Theo nodded toward the pair of siblings as Sophia climbed on his back and Ethan punched him in his gut.

"There are a couple of younger traders that ran away down the tunnel," Philip said.

"You want us to follow them?"

"Not now," Philip said as he shook his head. "If they really were younger, there's little chance they are the ringleaders."

"Where's Rose?" Theo glanced around. "I don't see her."

Roderick came barreling through, helping Sophia and Ethan finish off the last attacker. "She ran ahead after her horse to get Mary," he said. "And I haven't seen her since."

Theo glanced over at their attackers. Bruises were beginning to form on their faces, and many of them looked well beaten. "Captain," he called. "Watch over these traders. Bind them up and take them back out of the cave. King Derick's men should be able to come and gather them."

"What are we going to do?" Ethan asked.

"*Find Rose.*" Theo wiped the sweat off his face, hiding his concern.

"I'm here," Rose called.

Together, all of them turned around to look at her. Mary was on her shoulder, her wings giving off a soft bubble of growing light.

He nearly ran to her in relief. But he stopped the moment he saw her face. "What's wrong?"

Sophia came up to her, pushing past Theo, and gave her a hug. "Rose," she said. "What happened?"

"I got lost."

"I saw you disappear," Roderick said. "Was it the Wandering Caverns?"

"Must've been," Rose said, brushing off their concerns in an easy tone. "I apologize if I've worried you."

Theo saw her wring her hands, and he was only slightly comforted when she reached for the rosary beads he knew she wore under her sleeve. He had given her his rosary beads when they had returned to Rhone for her seventeenth birthday. While Theo doubted she used them for prayer, he took comfort in knowing that she carried them with her.

As the others began to talk with her, Theo noticed the expression Mary wore on her face. The small fairy was silent as her wings fluttered, and she took off from Rose's shoulder.

"Tell me about the attack," Rose said. "Did we get everyone?"

"Not everyone," Philip told her. "But the ones who ran away were the smart ones. They seemed young. I think Derick's forces can take over from this point. They were not too far behind us when we left."

"You managed to fight off a group of Magdust traders," Rose said. "There might be more. We should continue onward and keep looking."

"True," Philip said. "We didn't see any sign of Magdalina, anyway. It's possible we could still see her."

In the soft, colorful light of the cavern's atrium, Theo saw Rose's face pale. He was willing to bet that Rose was not telling them the whole story. He watched her as she began asking Philip and Ethan more questions, while Sophia tended to the horses, and Roderick and the other guards were binding up their newly-bound prisoners, preparing to take them out of the caverns.

Something is not right, Theo thought.

"Send Lannister back to the King," Rose said. "He's the lightest man we have. He'll be able to ride to the palace quickly. Captain, you and Roderick can stay with the men until they are arrested."

"Yes, my lady," Captain Locke replied. He bowed his head. "But please be careful as you make your way through the rest of the countryside. Bandits and traders are often reluctant allies in places such as this."

"I will be careful, Captain. You do the same."

Theo watched as the captain nodded and set out to do his assigned work. The older man never had a problem following Rose's orders, he thought. It was gratifying to know he was as reliable as he was.

As soon as the captain took his leave, while the others were getting themselves together, Theo took Rose's arm. "You're lying," he told her softly.

"And you're bothering me," Rose snapped.

"Something happened while you were gone. Tell me."

"You're paranoid." Rose tugged her arm free and stomped away from him. "And I have work to do."

"Rose."

She shook her head. "We have to get to Einish. We can still make it to O'Lin before too long if we hurry."

He sighed.

"Come on, Theo," Rose said. "Isra is waiting for us. I'm sure you'd love to see her."

"What's that supposed to mean?" Theo asked, surprised by her accusing tone.

Rose glanced over her shoulder at him, frowning. "Never mind. Now, let's go."

"I've never accused you of being ugly before, Rose," Theo said. "And no one in his right mind would. But this is coming awfully close."

"Well, it's good that I'm tired of hearing how beautiful I am, then," Rose retorted.

Theo said nothing else. He looked at Mary, who gave him a sympathetic look. He felt like following Rose, fighting with her until she admitted what it was she was keeping from him. But he knew it would only cause his relationship with Rose to be further fractured in the end.

Sophia called out to him from further down the trail.

"Theo?" Sophia called. "Can you help me?"

"What is it?" he asked, coming over beside her.

"This." Sophia held up a small object in her hands. It took Theo a moment to realize it was a pixie.

He had never seen a pixie before in his life, outside of drawings. He knew the pixies were a diverse race, with different languages and different physical traits. The one Sophia carried had a twiggish face, twisted and hard, almost as if he

91

had grown out of a tree like a branch. The pixie's large eyes were closed and his body was limp as Theo looked him over.

"Is he … okay?" Theo asked softly.

"I don't know," Sophia said. "I was hoping you could check."

Theo nodded and began looking for any sign of a pulse, hoping he would find any sign of life. The instant his finger touched the creature's neck, he felt a small amount of breath inhaling and exhaling from the body. It wasn't a pulse, he thought, but it was enough for him. "He's alive."

"Is he hurt?"

"Likely. We better tend to him. Are there anymore pixies around that you've seen?"

"No." Sophia shook her head. "Not yet, anyway. Ethan and I saw him crawl out of one of the caverns while we were fighting. I think he was hit with something while we were distracted with the traders. Ethan went down the side path some, to check for more."

"I'll go and get Ethan. He shouldn't wander off on his own. In the meantime, take extra good care of him, then," Theo instructed, pointing to the pixie in her hands. "We'll need to see if he can answer some questions for us."

"What if he was working with the Magdust traders?" Sophia still cuddled the small creature like a baby, but Theo knew for all her compassion, she had a right to question the pixie's motives.

"Go and get Mary," Theo said, brightening at the idea. A distraction for Mary could mean that he would get some time to see if Rose would tell him what happened while he had been fighting off the traders with the others. And, he added, trying to justify it, Mary would be able to make sure that the pixie did not cause them any trouble. "See if she can help with him. She might be able to use some of her healing mag-ic."

Sophia nodded and hurried off, while Theo went off in search of Ethan.

He walked into the side tunnel and felt a strong presence of magic. Theo's fingertips brushed against the wall, and he felt the tingle of magic.

Magdust.

"Ethan," he called. "Ethan, come back this way." A sense of foreboding came over him.

He breathed a sigh of relief when he saw his young companion appear only a few yards ahead of him.

"Theo," Ethan said. "You won't believe what I found here."

"I don't know about that," Theo said as he went over to stand next to Ethan.

There was a small crevice in the rock. Glancing through it, Theo saw a blueish glow. He looked through it and immediately felt a rush of sorrow.

The cave reeked of painful death. Theo was already praying for peace as he pushed through the small opening in the rock, and stepped into the cave opening.

Blue light washed over him instantly. It felt cool on his skin, and even through his armor, he could tell some time had passed since the death of the fairies.

Ethan stepped in behind him. "What is this?" he asked. "I don't like it."

"It's a death chamber," Theo told him. "The blue residue you see is from fairy blood."

"Fairies? Not pixies?"

Theo nodded. He looked around, careful to watch his step. He saw the old, dusty footsteps in the rocky dirt. "The traders must have brought them here after they captured them." He saw a cage in the corner, smashed in. He examined it closely.

Fairies were not supposed to like iron, he knew; that was part of the reason that almost all the steel used in making swords contained iron. The cage gleamed dark silver against the blueish glow.

"Theo, look."

At Ethan's startled gasp, Theo came over to stand beside Ethan.

"It's a spinning wheel," he said. "To make thread."

"Well, we have to keep Rose away from here for sure now," Ethan joked, his voice humorless. "The spindle is still on it."

"They were using the Magdust," Theo said examining the spinning wheel more closely. "Spinning it right into the yarn."

"Why?" Ethan asked. "Why not just consume it?"

"I don't know," Theo replied. "It's probably a mystery to people like you and me because we would never do this sort of thing in the first place. But that's a good question."

His thoughts went back to his own upbringing, where his mother had hung that tapestry in his house. Thad had mentioned that their mother might have found a way to force his father's hand in marriage, but things were starting to wear off by the time they had to leave their home. Was she able to use the Magdust in the tapestry to convince her father to stay? "Maybe it is easier to use by a human when it comes to granting wishes for things other than power."

Ethan did not seem to hear his speculation. "We should go back," he said. "Before someone gets worried about us."

Theo nodded slowly. "I'll leave a message for King Derick with Captain Locke," he said. "So he knows about this place."

ONCE UPON A PRINCESS

The two of them made their way back to the main trail. Ethan was quiet and sober, while Theo was contemplative. His heart ached for the fairies and their losses. How was it that humans were able to capture and kill them so easily? Theo wondered. It did not seem like the men they had fought were that powerful. They were missing something. But what? Mary could have told them easily if it was something she knew.

Theo knew the church's teachings on the fallen state of human beings and the rest of the world. It was not hard to imagine why people would do something as terrible, something that required the reality of the scene he had just left. Desire, power, magic … all of it held an allure to the fallen soul, and some souls could not help but search after such things.

"There you are."

Rose's voice might have been edged with impatience, but it still carried the same graceful song. Theo couldn't stop himself from smiling at her, even if it made her frown even more.

"Ethan," Rose said, "you shouldn't have gone off on your own. You're lucky we didn't end up losing you."

"Sorry," he said. "I was just doing a quick check for other pixies. How is the one Sophia and I found earlier?"

"Still unconscious," Rose said. "We'll have to see about getting him help once we arrive in Einish."

"I'll rig up a pallet for him," Ethan offered.

"Sophia said she could carry him. Mary's watching with her."

Ethan rolled his eyes. "Trust Sophia to find a way to have all the fun."

Theo came up beside Rose as Ethan sauntered back over toward his horse.

ONCE UPON A PRINCESS

"I need to leave some notes for the King," Theo told Rose. "There's a cave back there with a multitude of dead fairies inside."

Rose's eyes watered. "So we were too late."

"Considerably," Theo agreed sadly. "But the cave has been in use for some time."

"Did you find anything else?" Rose asked. "No more guards or traders or anything else?"

Theo shook his head, deciding not to mention the spinning wheel. "There might be more throughout the caverns," he said. "Tucked off to the side."

"Or just hid with other magic," Rose murmured. "What do you think? What should we do?"

"We have removed one band of Magdust traders," Theo said. "Let's keep an eye out for more, and take care of them if we see it."

"And if we don't find any more?"

"There's no need to go looking for more trouble, Rose," Theo replied with a smirk. "We always find enough of it on our own."

"So we should just keep going through the cave?"

"I think we can head out for Einish without worry. Didn't the king say he was going to send some of his own men to take care of this matter anyway?"

"Yes, he did."

"Then he will. So we can move onward." It was so tempting to tug on a lock of her hair as he had done many times before. It was something that always seemed to cheer her up. But Theo knew Rose was still upset with him, and it would be better if he kept their conversation focused on business. "Philip needs to get to his betrothed, after all."

Rose gave him the smallest hint of a smile. "You're right," she said. "Thank you."

Her hand reached out and gripped his for a brief moment. Theo did not allow himself to be happy over it; he knew Rose was only allowing them to reestablish their normal boundaries.

And if there was one thing he knew, it was that he did not want their normal relationship any longer. He wanted more.

ONCE UPON A PRINCESS

10

The first glimpse of Einish's grand palace in their port city was nothing short of breathtaking.

Literally breathtaking, Rose thought, as she finally came to the top of the mountain trail. Over the last day, from climbing out of the Wandering Caverns to climbing up a mountain, she was already tired. But the high mountain air seemed to slow her breathing.

She was not the only one who suffered from the high altitudes. The terrain had been hard on her horse, so she had dismounted several hours before, leading her mare and her company on foot. With the others following her example, their pace had slowed, but they were still making good time.

The view of the city, lingering in the distance, brightened her mood. "We're almost there," she called back. "I can see it from here."

Philip came up beside her, his horse nearly bumping into hers as he gazed at his home. "It'll be only another hour," he said. "The mountains around this part of the city are the last real challenge, and now that we're at the top, it's all downhill from now on."

Rose grinned. "And then we'll see Isra and my brother again."

"Oh, yes, I'd forgotten your brother will be there." Philip gave her an amused look. "I shouldn't have to worry about him, right?"

"He's here as your guest," Rose said. "I'm sure he will be the one who is worried."

"Is he the sort who gets overprotective of his sisters?" Philip asked. "Do you think he's anxious to meet me? I know I wasn't able to meet him when we were back in Rhone for your birthday."

"I think he'll only be worried for when you come," Rose said, "because it will be harder to get everything that he wants."

Philip laughed. "Oh, I get it. He's probably making himself right at home then?"

"More than right," Rose assured him. "He's into his creature comforts, but he can be very charming. So your servants will be running around all night, but he will be running them around with a smile. Even your notorious mother I've heard so much about might have a hard time telling him no."

"My only hope in this matter is that I have you with me, isn't it?"

Rose grinned. "Well, that and that Isra is there. But she might let him do what he wants, under the pretext of keeping up appearances."

"Well, then let's hope I have a full castle and staff to get back to."

"You mean your mother wouldn't order them to stay?"

"True enough." Philip kept in step with Rose as they continued on the path. He asked her more questions about Ronan and even some more about Isra, and that was when Rose confronted him.

"Why do you want to know so much about them so badly?" she asked. "You've met Isra, and you seem to know her better than I do some days. Ronan is not much like either of us, but there's no reason to think he wouldn't come to like you. You are a very likeable person."

"Thank you," Philip said. He smiled, and despite his thick beard, Rose was able to see the small dimple at the side of his cheek. "I'm glad you find me likable."

ONCE UPON A PRINCESS

"Of course. We have always been able to get along."

"Not always. You didn't like me much after I beat you in the joust back in Rhone."

Rose rolled her eyes. "You should know by now I'm used to winning. I haven't learned to be a good loser, and if that's the one thing I'm never going to learn, I'm okay with that."

Philip laughed. "Well, for what it counts, the feeling is mutual. I think you're very likable, too."

Rose felt her face turn red with embarrassment. "I do like you," she said, "and I hope you know I consider us friends."

"Of course." He gave her a wink. "The best of friends."

"Well, sort of. I don't think as a future monarch we can have a lot of friends like our subjects can, but—"

"You know I don't mean that," Philip said. He took her free hand in his. "You know I mean that we are more than just friends."

"What?" Rose stepped back. "No, we're not."

"Come on, Rose," Philip said. "We're going to be a part of each other's lives for a long time. You might as well just admit what's in your heart."

"What's in my heart?" Rose repeated.

"We're going to be a big, happy family one day."

Rose felt her embarrassment transform into fear. "No, we're not."

"Why not?" Philip asked. "You just said that we were friends, and I know for a fact we are more than friends."

"If you were really my friend, you would stop prattling on as if we were going to get married one day."

"Well, aren't we?" Philip asked.

"No!"

"Why not?"

"Because I'm not in love with you!" Rose glared at him. "And despite what you might think, you're not in love with me, either."

"Why aren't you in love with me?" Philip asked, looking wounded. "Is there someone else?"

"No!" Rose asserted, as her cheeks turned hot.

Philip gave her a teasing smile. "I think there's someone else."

"No," Rose reiterated desperately. "No there's not, because he shouldn't love someone like me, and I won't let him."

As soon as the words left her mouth, and she heard herself say them, Rose stilled. Anger, with fear, with sadness—all of it unleashed inside of her, as she realized she had revealed herself. She ducked behind her horse's face as she continued walking, her steps suddenly much stiffer.

"Are you alright?"

"Please," she said, loud enough Philip could hear her, "don't talk to me about this anymore."

"It wasn't really that hard to admit, was it?" Philip asked gently. "I've known about it since we met in Rhone."

She glanced back over at Philip, who was looking at her with a kind patience.

"Rose," he said, "you know that there is a tradition in Rhone that a suitor must complete an assigned task to grant the right to marry into the crown's family, right?"

Rose slowly nodded. "I hope you don't think that coming with me to the Serpent's Garden counts as a task," she said. "The ruler is the one who is supposed to assign the task in question."

"Well, Isra was the one who assured me that the task she gave me would count."

Rose narrowed her eyes at him suspiciously. "What makes you think I would give you my hand in marriage just because you came along with me and the rest of my crew? Isra can say what she pleases, but I won't consent to marry you for embarking on this task."

"I wasn't really concerned about your hand," Philip said.

"But why were you just—"

"My assigned task wasn't specifically to come along with you, even though I ended up doing so," Philip said. "I appreciated that Isra was happy to let me come, because I did want to have grand adventures on my own. It was hard to do that, you know, until my brother got married. When you meet my mother, I think you'll find out why."

"So you didn't want to marry me," Rose realized. "But why did you just do all that right now? With all the 'we are more than friends' speech, and how we're going to be 'one big, happy family' one day?"

"Why do you think, Rose?" Philip asked. "It's the same reason I've been provoking you and Theo since we left Rhone. My task was to get you to admit you were in love with him."

"What?" Rose stopped short in her tracks. Immediately, she glanced around to make sure that they were still far enough ahead of the others that they couldn't hear her panicked shrieking.

Philip nudged her along. "Come on, keep moving. This is just as awkward for me as it is for you. Theo's already looking like he's trying to find an excuse to get up here so he can cut in on my flirting. Of course, he never does, if he doesn't think you'll find his excuse believable."

Rose glanced back at Theo, only to see Philip was right. When Theo saw her look at him, he turned away, but not before she saw the frustration on his face.

"Next thing you know, he'll look for an excuse to throw me off the mountainside." Philip tugged on his horse's reins again. "I can't say I blame him. I'd probably do the same, if you were mine."

"I'm not his." Rose looked down her nose at Philip. "I don't belong to anyone."

"Well, he's certainly yours," Philip said. "I'd hate to think what he would do to me if he wasn't my friend, too."

"You're crazy," Rose said. "He knows, of all people, how I feel about love."

"And he is the one person, of all people, who is determined to get past the barriers you have in your heart."

Rose shook her head. "He won't."

"Well, I did get you to admit that you didn't have someone because you would never let him love you," Philip reminded her. "So there's that."

"Don't you see?" Rose asked. "I'm not going to marry any-one."

"Don't *you* see?" Philip countered. "If it wasn't for the curse, you would be free to do what your heart wants. And that includes admitting you love him."

"You said this was supposed to be awkward for you, too," Rose said, trying to ease out of the topic. "Tell me this. If you didn't come with me as your task, and if your task was in fact to get me to admit I was in love with … someone else … then why did you do it?"

"Why else?" Philip asked. "I'm in love with a princess of Rhone, indeed, Rose, even if it's not you, and I will happily set to accomplish what I can to make her happy."

"Isra." Rose rubbed her forehead. "Really? Didn't you *just* meet her what, nearly seven months ago? And weren't you only with her for *two days?* Who falls in love after only two days?"

"I can't explain it," Philip said. "I met her, and then … then everything just came together. We knew each other so well, and we'd only just met. It was like a dream."

"If it was a dream, how do you know it's real?" Rose retorted.

"That's how I know you've yet to let yourself fall," Philip said. "When it comes to love, you don't always know it's real outside how you feel. But sometimes you have to have faith in something before you see it. And then, all of sudden, you can see it."

"So you really do love her?"

"She stole my heart the first time we danced," Philip said. "Sometimes, when I have trouble sleeping, I relive that moment. I felt my heart slip out of my chest and fall right into her hands."

Rose briefly recalled how talented Philip was as a poet and, despite her concern, smiled. "And Isra loves you, too? So much that she sent you out on a special task to earn her hand?"

"Well, she was more like you about that," Philip admitted. "She told me about the tradition of the task, and told me if I wanted to prove myself true to her, she would give me a task to carry out."

"So she gave you the task of humiliating me," Rose muttered. "Nice."

"She loves you, Rose, for all she doesn't understand you." Philip reached out and patted Rose's shoulder. "I have no doubt that she wanted me to succeed, but it would also give me some time to prove myself worthy of her in other ways."

"Your letters." Rose shook her head again. "I thought you were pushing me to write to her more often just to annoy me and gain support from her. But you actually set out to please her."

"Yes. I want to make the engagement official."

"You might have to talk to King Stefanos about that," Rose said. "He's still the ruler of Rhone."

"It was your blessing I wanted," Philip said. "Despite all the trouble I have given you."

"Well, you have my blessing," Rose told him. "Really, you *are* my blessing. You had my respect early on. I think if you can earn that, you have a good chance of winning Isra's heart. She's the only one who should be free to give it to you. So if you are sure—"

"I am." There was no hesitation in Philip's voice. Rose felt the hard reality of jealousy, though more for Philip's certainty than for his constancy.

She smiled. "Well, if she is sure, I will sign the official engagement papers while I am here."

"Really?"

"Yes. But you will have to wait until she is older. She's only sixteen yet."

"I'm so grateful, Rose."

Rose laughed. "Don't look so surprised. I want someone who will be able to protect Isra from Magdalina and any other trouble, and someone who will love her more than anything else in the world. If what you say is true, and I have no reason to doubt you, then I should be fortunate you want to marry her."

"Thank you, Rose." Philip reached out and kissed her hand. "You are a wonderful sister."

"Only if my wonderful sister is eager to make it so," Rose reminded him.

"You said it yourself; if I can earn your respect, I can win her heart." He glanced behind him. "What about you? Are you going to tell Theo?"

"We're talking about you right now," Rose said, determined to keep away from that topic. "After all, we're almost to the castle. You should have some kind of speech or poem ready for Isra when you see her. I'll be happy to help you with that."

"Come on, Rose."

"Come on, Philip." Rose smirked. "I'm not that terrible at poetry, and hearing you put all my sister's charms into stanzas might let me see just how much you know her, and just how much you love her."

"You're a tough opponent, Rose," Philip said. "I don't envy you. You have to fight yourself a lot, don't you?"

It was a light jab, but Rose felt the sting of truth inside of it. Rose frowned at him. "Stick to poetry for now, Philip. Consider that your first piece of advice from your new sister."

11

Theo watched as Rose and Philip chatted together in front of the castle as several grooms approached and began taking their baggage and their horses to the royal stables. He had watched them as they made their way down the mountain, and he had felt the pain of Rose's rejection as she turned away from him once more.

I should be used to it by now.

But, he added to himself, it at least looked like Rose was doing better than she was when they were in the cavern. She had not had an easy night, as they camped once they arrived at the base of the mountain. Earlier that morning, he had woken up to find her restless and distressed. But when he approached her, she had gone back to her pallet, immediately convinced she wanted to try to sleep more than she wanted to talk with him.

From where he was, he could see she was happy.

And he was happy for her.

Or so he told himself.

"Rose!"

Theo glanced up to see Isra, running down from the castle steps. She held her skirts high in one hand, and he could see her black hair was tumbling free from its pins as she waved hi.

"Hi, Isra!" Rose called.

"Isra!" Philip bellowed, cupping his hands around his mouth as he greeted her. "My belovéd!"

Theo watched, confused, as Philip ran out to meet Isra.

Ethan came up beside him, his eyes bright as he held onto his satchel. "Do you think Isra will want to listen to me play my harp tonight?" he asked. "I might have to tune it, but it shouldn't take me long to play a song or two for her."

"Probably not tonight," Theo said.

"Aw." Ethan pouted. "I was able to fix it up really nice at the other palace. And I figured Isra would be able to help me out with some of the more complicated chords. It's been a long time since Penelope taught me. I don't want to forget before I see her again."

"I'm sure you'll find some time to let Isra help you," Theo assured him. "But it's late enough as it is. The sun is going down, and Philip still has to meet with his mother. She's the one who is really in control of this castle. We'll need to be on her good side if we're going to be able to take care of our work while we're here."

"I know Isra and Philip are supposed to be engaged," Ethan said. "I didn't know there were other things we have to watch for."

"While we're here, I'd like to see about arranging a meeting with Ambassador Rolez," Theo said, forcing himself to stop watching Rose as she watched Philip catch Isra by the waist and circle her around.

He could not forget that he had a mission. They all had a mission. Even though they had fulfilled their promise to Derick, they still had to find Magdalina and Everon, and Theo knew the Magdust trade was somehow connected to everything. He needed more information, and the man who had been so insistent on the good fortune the tapestry would bring to Queen Juliette's children was a logical priority.

"Who's he?" Ethan asked.

"The man who gave that tapestry to Juliette," Theo replied. "I want to know where he got it, and if he knows anything else about it."

"Because of the spinning wheel we found?" Ethan asked quietly.

"Partially. But I have other reasons as well." Theo did not want to elaborate on his family history to Ethan. Both Ethan and Sophia had enough experience of their own when it came to family concerns. They had been neglected and abused by their father, and ever since Rose and Theo had rescued them, Theo had tried to keep his own dark past from them. He was glad when Sophia called out to him.

"What is it?" he asked, coming up to her.

"The pixie," Sophia replied. "He's starting to wake up."

Theo came over to the small bundle strapped to Sophia's saddle. He watched as the large eyes of the pixie blinked open.

Instantly, the pert little face twisted into a painful, bitter scowl. "Who are you?" the creature demanded. "Where am I?" He sat up and grabbed at his left leg. "And why is my leg aching like the devil?"

Theo stepped up. "You were injured when we found you in the cavern in the forest of Einish. We have brought you to the city so we could see to your wounds."

"I am free?" The pixie's large eyes were suddenly very wet with emotion instead of pain.

"Free from what?" Sophia asked.

"Where is my master?" The pixie asked. "I need to find my master." He sank back into despair.

"We're not sure," Theo replied. "What is your master's name?"

"Master Mick," the pixie answered. He tried to sit up, but Sophia held him down. As he protested against her concern, Theo looked back over to see Rose was now talking with

Philip and Isra. She was probably going over the story, he thought.

Mary came up beside him. "I can see if his master is alive," she said. "He's obviously too weak to use his magic, but I can check for it."

"Check for what?" Ethan asked.

"When a pixie has a master, there's a mark on his palm," Mary said. "You can see it with revealing magic."

"Let's see if he'll let you," Theo said. He faced the pixie. "What is your name?"

"Bachas," the creature replied. "I am a native of Crystal Lake. My master saved my life, and I was bound to him through a life debt."

"That's how it usually happens," Mary muttered. "You know that can be faked, right?"

Bachas blinked at Mary, before his face contorted with disgust. "You're a fairy," he spat. "Your kind was the reason I was in danger in the first place."

"Still, she has nothing to do with your personal situation. And she can see if you are still bound by your oath," Theo said. "Mary, check his palm."

"No!" Bachas twisted away from her. "I won't let a dirty fairy touch me."

Mary shot Theo a hard look. He glanced at Ethan and Sophia and gave them a quick signal. Together the three of them grabbed one of the pixie's small limbs.

"Go, Mary," Theo said, torn between feeling sympathetic for Bachas and angry at him, as the small creature kicked at his face relentlessly. "We got him."

"Stop twitching!" Mary shouted. She grabbed his hand and he cried out in pure, angry terror. A flash of light sparked,

ONCE UPON A PRINCESS

followed by a rush of energy. Mary backed up and grabbed her hand. "You stung me!"

Bachas grimaced. "Small reward for my trouble."

"Are you okay, Mary?" Ethan asked.

Sophia turned on Bachas. "You've got some nerve hurting our friend! If we hadn't taken care of you, you could have died."

"I wouldn't have died," Bachas insisted, but Theo was certain he saw a small amount of remorse at Sophia's chiding.

Or maybe fear, he thought. Bachas had to realize he was still too weak to get too far away if he tried to run. And with a fairy and weapons nearby, Theo had a feeling Bachas knew he could easily get in further trouble.

Mary fluttered up beside him. "I didn't see any seal," she said. "But if he's powerful enough to burn me, he'll be able to see it himself."

Bachas stuck his tongue out at her, but he did check his right hand. A moment later, he was struggling not to cry.

"So it's gone?" Sophia asked. "You're free?"

"Yes." Bachas blinked his large eyes up at her. "I am free now. My awful master is dead."

No one said anything for a long moment, with Bachas only letting his tears fall. "I can return to my family," he said happily, and then he stopped. "Assuming they are still alive."

"Can you tell us what happened to you?" Theo asked. "We have a few questions about what was going on in the caverns as well."

Bachas hesitated. "I don't want to help any fairies," he said. He added, "Or anyone who is working with them."

"We might be able to help you get back to your family," Theo said. "We have friends here. Someone can take you back. We can also get some medicine for you, to help you grow stronger. We can also provide supplies to you, if you need it. Believe me, we face a bigger foe than a fairy.”

“Who is that?” Bachas snorted. “That wicked fairy ruler, Magdalina?”

“Yes.”

Bachas stared at him for a long moment before he laughed. “Well, you’re on the losing side,” he said. “She’s managed to hang onto her power for years, even after she was kicked out of the fairy realm by Oberan.”

“The King of the Aragonian Fairies?” Mary asked.

“Who else? Stupid fairy.” Bachas scowled at her.

“Hey,” Mary snapped, “I don’t know much about him for good reason. He’s not *my* ruler!”

“Doesn’t matter. If Magdalina was able to find a place to take refuge in your world, it’s your own fault for letting her.”

“We want to stop her,” Theo said. “After all the help we’ve given you, by setting you free and offering to get you back home, won’t you help us some? All we need are some answers.”

“I’m tired, and my leg aches,” Bachas said, yawning. “Maybe in the morning. If I’m alive. I don’t see any reason to trust any of you.”

“You can trust me,” Theo said. “I was raised in the church and I know the demands of the priesthood.”

“But you’re not a real one,” Bachas pointed out. “God’s power won’t protect you like it would protect a real priest.”

“Priests are protected from your magic?” Ethan asked. “I didn’t know that.”

“There’s a reason we stay away from the churches,” Bachas said. “It’s harder to make mischief there.”

“We still protected you,” Sophia said. “I carried you in my arms as we walked over the mountain. Ethan was the one who made up a sling for you so you would be comfortable when I got tired."

In the darkening light, Theo thought he saw Bachas' cheeks turn a dull shade of gray. Sophia was making him uncomfortable, he realized. Maybe the pixie had a soft spot for ladies.

"Fine." Bachas eventually gave up. "But I want to eat first."

Theo smiled. "I think we can arrange that. Let me go and speak to Isra."

"She is waiting for you, by the look of it," Ethan said. "She keeps looking over this way."

Theo craned his neck, looking over at where Philip and Isra were talking with Rose. He watched as Rose hugged her sister, obviously glad to see her safe.

As she held onto Rose, Isra caught his eye. She waved at him, beckoning him to come over.

"Well, I guess you're right, Ethan," Theo said. "I'm being summoned. Stay here and keep watch over Bachas. Make sure he doesn't try to hurt Mary or run away."

"I will," Ethan promised. He lowered his voice, "Will you ask Isra about letting me play the harp for her?"

"You have my word," Theo promised, before he made his way over toward Isra.

Rose's younger sister sometimes made him wonder what Rose might have been like if not for Magdalina's curse. She was smart and insightful, and she knew how to wield her wit as sharp as a weapon. She was also much more cheerful—or at least she was when she was around him.

He noticed that, as she stood next to Philip, she looked like she was having the time of her life.

"Theo!" she cheered. "I'm so glad to see you. I've saved all your letters since we last met."

Rose rolled her eyes. "It wasn't that long ago, Isra."

"My life might as well have begun again, Rose," Isra told her in her most demure tones, while she leapt into Theo's arms. "It's nice to see you again, brother," she whispered into his ear. "I have missed you."

"It's nice to see you again, too," Theo said.

"I am really happy everyone is here," Isra told him. "I worry about you, you know."

Theo let her go, carefully setting her back down on her feet. "There's no need to do that."

Isra's kind eyes blinked up at him, the dying sunlight transforming the amber to gold. "Rose makes everything more difficult," she said, loudly enough to let Rose hear. "That's why I wanted you to write to me. So I could interrupt her monopoly on your time."

"Is that why?" Rose crossed her arms. "I thought it was just to annoy me and make me feel like someone else was trying to keep tabs on my every movement, just like they did when we were younger."

Isra gave her a brilliant smile before she turned back to Theo. "Come and walk with me," she said. In a lower voice, she added, "It'll make Rose upset."

Theo did not argue with Isra, but he did ask, "Why do you think it would be good to upset her?"

"So she will be less angry about the party Philip's mother is planning for us at the end of the week."

"Oh, I see." Theo smiled. "She won't like to hear that."

"No, she won't," Isra agreed. "I know she wants to get home quickly, but Philip's doing so much for our group of friends. I feel like we should try to make his mother happy. She is an older lady and suffers from the vapors a lot."

"A lot?"

"Let's just put it like this. If I ever suffer from the vapors, please kindly don't take me seriously unless I am dying."

Theo chuckled. "So how many false alarms has there been since you arrived?"

"Plenty," Isra said through gritted teeth. "The Dowager Queen, Utopa, is quite dramatic."

"You think Rose will like her?"

"Tolerably."

"That's all?"

Isra shrugged. "That's all I need, right?"

Theo paused. "Are you actually going to go through with the wedding?" he asked. "I thought you were lying about it. You said you needed to confess some terrible things in your letter."

"I know. I think I forced Philip's hand," Isra said. "I mean, we talked about marriage when we first met—"

"What?" Theo's eyes widened. "Why?"

"Because. We just … fell in love." Isra blushed, but she held her ground as he stared at her. "Come on, Theo. I expect this sort of response from Rose, but not you."

"He didn't tell me."

"I told him not to." Isra tightened her grip on his arm. "I didn't want Rose to punish him or try to scare him off. And I thought it was prudent when he went off with you guys, because I thought it was a very small way I could help protect you. I had no idea I would be off on my own adventure, if you would even call this an adventure." She nodded toward the high castle towers before her.

"You don't think this is very adventurous?" Theo asked.

"No. Dealing with actual dragons seems infinitely more stimulating than dealing with my future mother-in-law and her love for etiquette. You would think she and Ms. Winston,

ONCE UPON A PRINCESS

my old governess, were long-lost sisters! They chitter-chatter together every day for tea and it is appalling to watch them. Especially when they are criticizing me, and thinking themselves the better for it."

"I've got to admit, I'm looking forward to meeting the Dowager," Theo said. "Between delaying Rose, throwing fits and throwing parties, and being compared to dragons, I'm curious to see her."

"Her fangs are probably not as visible," Isra warned. "You might regret your enthusiasm."

Theo patted her arm. "There's no need to accustom me to disappointment, Isra. I'm well taught, from traveling so long with Rose."

12

"I don't see why you're so upset, Rose," Isra said as she sat down next to the open window in Rose's room. "At least we're safe for the moment. And it's just a week."

"In a week, we could make it to Rhone and back," Rose muttered as she threw her bag of clothes on the bed before her.

"Come on. This is a chance for you to relax. I know for a fact that you didn't enjoy yourself at Crystal Lake."

Rose's temper flared at the mention of Crystal Lake. Did Theo tell Isra what had happened at the hot springs, when he'd seen her at the pool? She struggled to keep her voice even as she asked, "Is that what you were talking about with Theo?"

"Does it bother you he'd rather talk to me about certain things?" Isra asked, her eyes wide and innocent.

"I just don't understand why you're so dependent on him," Rose scoffed. "That's all."

"You depend on him."

"He is my confidant and one of my knights," Rose said. "He's nothing important like that to you."

"He's my friend, and I consider him as another brother," Isra said. "And you're just horrible if you think that he is just some knight or counselor to you. He's the one who changed your life, Rose. He's the one who set you free."

"I'm not free," Rose snapped. "I'm still cursed."

"Cursed, yes, but at least you know about it," Isra pointed out. "Don't you ever wonder what would have happened if you never went crying into the chapel that day? You would have grown up as this naïve, innocent pawn doomed to a fate

117

no one could tell you about. You would have been pampered and courted and married off, if the King could find someone. That's just the best case scenario, too. At worst, the King and Queen would have made up a tower where, once you pricked your finger on the spindle, they could loving lay you down and allow citizens to parade through the room once a year as if it were some kind of holy political pilgrimage."

"You certainly thought it all out, did you?" Rose laughed.

Isra shrugged. "It sounds like a story of some sort."

"The awful kind."

"I won't argue with you there." Isra turned to face the window, where the cool evening air carried the scent of the nearby bay.

"I don't want to argue with you, even if I think I still would have found out about my curse," Rose said. She sighed. "I thought about what you said to me last time we were together. And you were right. I pushed a lot of people away, including you. I would like us to be friends."

"We always were," Isra assured her. "But I want more communication before you make decisions."

"You mean like how you agreed we would all stay for your big fancy engagement party?" Rose asked.

"That one doesn't count," Isra replied proudly. "Utopa made that call. I didn't have a lot of room to disagree. I mean, I'm fearing for my life here, Rose. Don't tell me you wouldn't protect me from Utopa as much as you would from King Stefanos."

"The King would just imprison you. Utopa is insistent on throwing you a party."

"When you meet her tomorrow, you'll see what I mean when I say it's hard for me to disagree with her."

"My life is not dependent on following her orders," Rose said. "I'll have to see what she's made of."

"Theo told me that it would be best for you and your traveling companions to stay here for a while anyway," Isra said.

"Really?" Rose sat down on her bed. "What reason did he give for that? My poor health? My inability to rest? My endless irritation?"

"Well, he said he wanted to talk to some ambassador while we were here. Something about a tapestry?"

Rose immediately felt shamed. She had forgotten about all about the tapestry she had seen at Derick and Juliette's castle. "Oh, right," she said. "There is that matter we have to sort out."

"I want to help you while we're here," Isra said. "So get some rest. Tomorrow, you can tell me all about this investigation, and we can help the others with that pixie they brought."

"The pixie?" Rose briefly recalled what looked like a sleeping log on the back of Sophia's saddle.

"His name is Bachas, and he does not like fairies at all. Mary's placed a spell on him to protect us from any of his harmful magic. It's a good thing she was there when he woke up. Pixies can be tricky creatures from what I've learned from here."

"You learned about pixies here?"

"We don't have practically any in Rhone," Isra said. "The fairyfolk we do have seem to have a grudge against them or something. They're more territorial than we realized."

"Well, I guess it's no wonder Magdalina wants our kingdom so badly," Rose said. "She told me that Lucia was supposed to be our first Queen."

Isra frowned. "When did she say that? I don't remember her saying anything about Lucia's legend at your birthday party."

Mary fluttered into the room before Rose could answer. Behind her was Isra's fairy, Fiona, who was also Mary's cousin. "That's because she told her while we were in the cave in the forest," Mary said.

"I didn't want you to tell anyone," Rose reminded her.

"Fiona and I have been discussing it," Mary explained. "We have been trying to find some answers for you, Rose, and I can't do that on my own. I am a younger fairy, don't forget. I don't know as much as someone like Fiona or Juana might know."

Fiona tapped her wings together thoughtfully. "And I do need all the details to be able to offer my best advice, darling Princess," she said.

Rose rolled her eyes. *What sorts of things people say to themselves in order to feel like they are not gossiping!*

"You mean you've talked to Magdalina again?" Isra asked. "While you were out in the caverns on your way here?"

"It's nothing," Rose said. "She did tell me a few things."

"Like what?"

Like how you are my half-sister. Rose did not want to say anything. "I can't tell you now, Isra. I need to verify what she said. You know Magdalina. She's all curses and riddles, and she only cares for herself."

"I guess so." Isra shook her head. "But as soon as you verify things, I want to know."

"Believe me," Rose said, "you'll find out if what she said was the truth or not soon enough."

It might be the reason the King is more than happy to imprison you and Ronan along with our mother.

Rose sighed. "There are so many things we need to find out, I'm tired just thinking of them all."

"Well, let me let you get some rest." Isra smiled. "Philip and I are going to take a walk on the battlements before bed," Isra said. "And then Theo asked if I would go and visit Sophia and Ethan. Ethan has a surprise for me, apparently. How sweet is that?"

"What is the plan for tomorrow?"

"Reception's before breakfast," Isra said, "where you'll officially meet Utopa. And wear a dress, please, Rose! She will have a fainting spell if she sees you in your knight's clothing."

"Fine," Rose replied bitingly. "What else?"

"I know we're going to go on a tour throughout the city," Isra said. "I've already mentioned this to Theo, and he agreed we should all go together."

"What? Why?"

"So you can find that ambassador," Isra answered.

"You tell Theo next time you talk with him I'm the one who is in charge."

"Rose, please. He's allowed to have his say. And it's not like he would do something to displease you. I can't imagine he likes getting you to yell at him all the time. No wonder he has to pray so often. He'd been insane otherwise."

Rose sat back on her hands, silently reminding herself that it was frowned upon for someone to choke her sister. As her fingers curled into her palms, she felt the rosary beads Theo had given her rest on her wrist. She took a deep breath as Isra listed off the rest of the coming day's projected activities.

"Then, I figure Philip and I can do enough things together that we can provide you some cover, so you can ask your questions around town and see if there is anything you can do about the Magdust trade and find that ambassador."

"I guess I have to wait for Lannister to return from Derick's palace with some news before we continue on to Rhone," Rose admitted.

"See? Why don't you just relax. For the moment, Magdalina can't hurt you. And I got a letter from the Queen Mother just last week, saying while she is still in prison, she is doing fine and things are mostly alright. So we have done what we can today."

Rose shifted onto the comfort of her mattress. It was nice to have Isra around, she thought, if for no other reason Isra could make her believe it was possible to forget about worrying. For some time, anyway.

"Okay," Rose said. "Alright. You win. We'll stay. I'll get some rest. We'll be fine."

"That's the spirit," Isra said. "Now, if you don't mind, I'm going to go and meet Philip."

"Take Juana and Mary," Rose ordered. "If you're really engaged, I'm going to treat it as such. So you need chaperones."

Isra giggled. "If it will help you sleep better, Rose. But there's really no need to worry about it. Ronan is going to join us. He wanted to make sure he could talk to Philip where, if he needed to throw him off something, he would have the opportunity to indulge himself."

Rose waited until she was alone in the room before she replied, "I doubt that will help me sleep better."

If anything, knowing Ronan will be there makes me even more nervous.

Still, she smiled. She was looking forward to seeing her brother again.

Half-brother.

Rose shrugged off Magdalina's words, and settled into her covers.

While she was able to relax in the borrowed bed, and she was able to believe Isra was right about the castle's security, Rose knew there were still too many questions running around inside of her head for her to fall asleep.

What did Theo tell Isra about their time at Crystal Lake? Would they be able to find the ambassador who had given Juliette the tapestry, and what did he say that made her so anxious to get rid of it? What was she going to say to her father when she saw him again? How would she defend Isra and Ronan from him, especially if they were her half-siblings?

Was she really going to be able to defeat Magdalina?

Too many questions, Rose thought. Not enough answers. Or maybe too many possibilities.

It seemed like hours had passed before she finally fell into a fitful sleep.

13

Theo also found himself awake, trying to answer lingering questions. He kept wondering what Rose had seen in the caves. He was determined to find a way to get her alone, so he could coax the answer from her at last.

His chance to do just that came shortly after breakfast finished up. It had been a lively, cheery breakfast, where Utopa, the Dowager Queen of Einish, nearly had a fit of the vapors when Rose wanted to talk business.

Theo had to swallow a laugh at the sight of Philip's mother as she finally agreed to have the contract for their engagement drawn up that very day, on the condition that Rose meet with her later to discuss the details in private. It was clear she had been appalled by Rose's manners, but she was determined to secure an alliance with Rhone.

The rest of the kingdom already seemed to be in agreement, he thought, as he sat with Rose, Isra, and Philip in the royal carriage.

As the rumors and gossip began to flow from room to room, and room to courtyard, Isra and Philip were prepared to go out on their tour of the city.

Theo had the others stay behind, so he could have some time alone with Rose as they sneaked off to go looking for Ambassador Rolez.

"So, what do you think?" Rose asked him, as she settled into the seat of the high coach beside him. They were on a carriage ride throughout the city, and even though they had just set out, Rose was already eager to escape.

Theo looked down to where Rose was looking. Isra and Philip were below, still waving to the people of Einish who had come to see their Prince and his betrothed bride set off on their tour through O'Lin. There was a large crowd, but there were plenty of guards around, all of them working to keep back the crowd's enthusiasm.

"I think you managed to throw Utopa off quite a bit at breakfast," Theo replied. "The outfit was a nice touch."

"She didn't make me change," Rose said, glancing down at her new dress, which was much neater than the one she had been wearing earlier. "She 'strongly suggested' it, but I did this myself."

"I think it's safe to say she knows you are not going to follow her lead by now," Theo said. "Especially after breakfast and how you managed to run the negotiations."

"I think she's out of practice," Rose said. "She didn't do a very good job at the start. And she easily could have called me out on some of my own shortcomings or double standards. After all, I was the one who insisted on protocol at the end, but didn't care for it at all until then."

"She's smart enough to know Rhone is a good match for Philip. It helps because he sincerely seems to like her enough to want to marry her."

Rose wrinkled her nose. "They both admitted to me that they're in love. Can you believe that? After only two days of knowing each other, and then almost seven months apart?"

Theo smiled and nodded, but inwardly he thought of his brother. Thad had told him before he knew Theo was at least half in love with Rose when he'd first met her, the time she had punched him in the nose. Some part of him wondered if he knew the exact moment he had fallen in love with Rose, and the other part knew it was pointless to try figuring it out after so many years.

"Love is mysterious to the people outside any relationship," he finally said.

"I guess so," Rose agreed.

Theo decided it was best to start distracting her. "Let's talk about how we're going to find Ambassador Rolez," he said.

Rose nodded. "Philip said he vaguely remembers him," she said. "If he sees him, he said he'll point him out to us as we go around to the different stops along the tour."

"Isra told me that they'll be stopping at many places, so I thought it might be better for us to slip away the first chance we get." Theo glanced back down at Isra and Philip, as they continued to wave at the people. "We might be able to save a lot of time by searching for him on our own."

"I'm okay with leaving once we get to the market," Rose said. "There are some dignitaries' houses they have to stop at first for some reason or another, but once we make to the market, we should be able to find out where the ambassador lives, or where he might be."

"I just hope he's in the country," Theo said. "I might want answers, but I don't want to travel all the way back to the Romani territory to get it. Or even further out."

"Agreed." Rose shook her head. "I hope this doesn't take too long."

"We have some time this week to find him," Theo reminded her.

"We have other problems to attend to," Rose said. "This is just one of the easier ones to solve."

It was an hour later when the carriage finally pulled up to the market, and Theo and Rose were able to slip out while Isra and Philip stepped out and started waving again.

"This seems demeaning," Rose said, as she watched Isra and Philip from around the corner of a nearby building. "Not to mention it takes forever."

"Traditions here differ from those of Rhone," Theo replied in a neutral tone. Unlike Rose, he had been grateful for all the time in the carriage. Isra had been able to point out several of the nobles and their residencies, and when they had stopped, Isra had used her charm to smooth over their audience—which, much to Rose and Theo's chagrin, was sorely needed, because many of the nobles mistook Rose for Isra, and even the ones who did not were caught staring at Rose enough that it was extremely uncomfortable—while asking indirect questions about Ambassador Rolez.

Rose wrinkled her nose. "I still like Rhone's better."

"Yes," Theo mused, "because it's just more convenient for one person to complete a monumental task than it is for the engaged couple to go around and greet their people."

Rose gave him a reluctant smile. "I guess so," she said.

"Your father had to complete a task for your mother," Theo reminded her. "I'm sure he would have appreciated this much more."

Rose made a face at the mention of her father. "Maybe it's more of a matter of how you always want what you can't have."

Theo was tempted to ask her what she would want to do if she ever got engaged, but he decided he did not want to know the answer.

"Well, let's get moving," Rose said. "That last duchess lady or whoever she was said that Rolez was not a native of Einish. He was an ambassador to Einish from Aragon."

"His townhouse is supposed to be around here," Theo said. "I'm trying to figure out which way is right of the town center. Her instructions were not the clearest."

"That's being kind," Rose said. "I'm amazed you were able to follow her at all, with all those stories she told in between her instructions."

"You get used to that, traveling around the world," Theo said, unable to stop him from tugging on a lock of her hair in play.

She didn't seem to remember she was supposed to hate it, so he took her arm. "Come on, let's go this way."

"I can walk myself," Rose grumbled.

"You look like a lady," Theo said. "And you're too pretty to be here by yourself. If you're with me, there's a smaller chance people will bother us."

"You're not so scary," Rose replied with a laugh. "I doubt you'll be able to scare off all the potential suitors."

"Then you'll just have to convince them all that you already belong to me."

He felt Rose stiffen as he said it, but when she laughed a moment later, he relaxed.

She batted her eyes up at him, pretending to flirt. "Is that so, darling?"

Theo grinned. "You have always valued an efficient plan, Rose."

"Don't you know me so well?" Her eyes lost their flirtatious edge as she looked up at him.

"I do," he told her, his tone much more husky than he had intended.

Rose shifted away from him, before she suddenly pointed at a building. "There's the city council building," she said.

ONCE UPON A PRINCESS

"That's the banner of Einish that the old lady was talking about. We're supposed to turn down this street."

She tugged him down the street, and they found themselves at a bazaar, a trader's outpost.

"There are so many things here," Rose said.

"After traveling through the mountains and countryside, I feel like this is a little surreal," Theo remarked. "Look over there. There's a shop from Maltia."

"I wonder if the shopkeeper knows Felise?" Rose pondered, craning her neck to see over the crowded alleyway.

Thinking of the older man who had overseen their care while they were stuck on the island, Theo shrugged. "Couldn't hurt to ask," Theo said. "Felise did tell us he often traded with any number of people in Maltia City."

"I see a shop with goods from Aragon," Rose said. "Maybe we should check there? To see if their ambassador found that tapestry from here?"

"That's a good idea," Theo said. "I didn't even think of it from that angle."

"Me either, until I saw it." Rose slipped through the various lines of people, still clinging to him, as she made her way over to the seller's table.

As they approached the shop, Theo had a hard time keeping his laughter to himself. The seller was an older man, with only a small streak of silver in his beard and at the edges of his hairline; it was clear he had been a seller for a long time, but while he had seen all manner of things before, Rose clearly managed to awe him considerably.

"Good morning," he called, heralding them with an excited energy. "What can I do for you, My Lady? Such a beauty as you deserves only the finest available. It is no coincidence that you have found your way to my shop."

ONCE UPON A PRINCESS

"Oh, I agree," Rose said, giving the owner a wide-eyed, innocent look. "I came here looking for something I've desperately wanted for ages now."

"Far be it from me to keep a lady from her desire," the man said, taking her free hand and gallantly kissing it. He was unable to take his eyes off of Rose. "My name is Enrique, and I am at your service, My Lady."

"Thank you," Rose said, trying to step back from the man's grip. She turned and patted Theo's arm. "My husband here is a good man and he has promised to buy me a very special tapestry."

"Your husband?"

Theo tried not to look too shocked as the older man sized him up. He could see the second the man resigned himself to Rose's claim; he had a feeling any prices that Enrique was going to offer before had just jumped significantly.

"Yes," Rose assured him. "My darling husband here promised me a grand tapestry of Queen Lucia. It was my favorite legend as a child, and after hearing Queen Juliette has one, I knew I just had to find one."

"You have excellent taste," Enrique said. "At least in goods." He glanced at Theo again, as if to condemn her choice in men.

Rose stayed focused on the tapestry. "I know Queen Juliette got her tapestry of Queen Lucia from Ambassador Rolez," she said. "I was hoping you would have one in stock, or you would be able to point me in the right direction."

"For a good price," Theo added, hoping to win some favor with the man.

Enrique arched a brow at him.

Okay, I did not win him over.

Rose seemed to realize this too. She let go of Theo's arm and took Enrique's hand. "Please, sir, you have to help me."

Enrique only had to look into her large, cerulean eyes before he crumbled. "I'm so sorry, My Lady," he said. "I do not have any in stock. I do not carry any tapestries of Queen Lucia."

Rose pouted.

"But," he said, "I do know where Ambassador Rolez bought his. He had a sister who was a duchess in the Aragonian court. He bought the tapestry on the way home from her funeral."

"Oh, I'm sorry to hear of his loss," Rose said, truly compassionate.

"He was very close to his sister, and so he rightly was. She was a very dear lady, trapped in a political marriage," Enrique said.

"You knew her?" Rose asked.

"Of course. She practically lived here. He went to go and bury her in their ancestral home."

"And the tapestry?"

"Shh … there is a weaver who lives in Rhone," he said, whispering. "She is from a family of weavers. Her name is Annalora, and she is the last remaining weaver who will do special tapestries such as the one you seek."

"Annalora?" Theo repeated. He held his breath as he asked, "Did she have a sister named Eleanora?"

"So the rumors go," Enrique replied, clearly forgetting he was supposed to object to Theo in light of the glory of sharing gossip. "I know Eleanora is gone. She and her husband were ambushed by a pack of hostile fairies just as they were going to visit Annalora. She has been distraught since then. Now, she only takes on special commissions."

Theo said nothing. It was so strange, he thought, to hear his parents' deaths described in such a matter-of-fact tone. It was just as strange as hearing his aunt was not only still alive, but she was still apparently working in the Magdust trade.

Rose did not seem to realize Theo was in shock. "Maybe Ambassador Rolez picked up an extra one while he was passing through Rhone," she said. "Can you tell us where we might be able to find him?"

"His townhouse is not far. But he is not receiving visitors," Enrique said. "He has only just returned from his sister's funeral, not even a week ago."

"Please," Rose entreated. "Please tell me. I will be content to write to him."

"Oh, My Lady, I cannot say no to you," Enrique told her. He took a hold of her hand again and squeezed it as he gave her the directions to the ambassador's house.

"Thank you," Rose murmured politely. She extracted herself from his grip and gave him a smile. "You have been most helpful."

She grabbed onto Theo's arm once more, and hurried away.

"You can slow down some," Theo told her, stumbling a bit at the sudden lurch in his steps. "It's not like you're trying to lose me. After all, I am your husband." He shot her a teasing grin.

"Ugh, please," Rose said. "That guy was creepy. I'm going to have to wash my hands extra thoroughly."

"Even if he was enchanted with you, at least he was able to be of some help."

"So?" Rose said. "I don't like it when people like him fawn over me like I'm some horse at an auction. Flirting with people like that makes my skin crawl. From now on, I'm just going to use straight intimidation."

"I'd prefer it, too," Theo admitted. "I know it makes you uncomfortable."

"Well, you're right; at least we got the information we need, for now, anyway."

"Even if Enrique is right, and he's not receiving visitors? How will we find a way to ask him questions?"

"I guess we'll see him at Isra and Philip's party," Rose said. "Any good foreign diplomat would not dare to miss an event like that."

"So that inconvenient party might be good for something after all?"

"Stop teasing. You know I hate it when you do that."

"And I know you're lying when you say that," Theo told her. He hesitated briefly. He was tempted to say, "Just like I knew you were lying about what happened in the cavern," but he knew it was too soon.

And, he had to admit, he was not willing to risk her temper. He was enjoying the day with Rose. They were alone in a crowded city, where Rose was comfortable enough with him that she was pretending he was her husband.

That fantasy alone was enough to intoxicate him into staying silent.

For the moment, he tightened his arm as it wound around hers and led her down through the bustling streets. Soon, one of the shops caught his eye.

"Hey, come over here," he said, as he pulled her further down the streets of the bazaar.

"What is it?" Rose asked. "Is it food?"

"Why? Are you hungry?"

"I didn't bring food with me for once."

"Really?"

"Come on, don't give me that look," Rose huffed. "I'm wearing a dress. It doesn't have pockets or anything."

"I could have carried something for you." Theo patted his own belt. "I have plenty of room to tie on traveling packets."

"Well, now you'll have to settle for buying me something," Rose told him.

"No need for subtlety, Rose," Theo said, drawing out some of the coins he'd tucked away. "We'll get some food for you in a moment. First, I want to check out this shop up here."

"Which one?"

Theo pointed to the small store where flowers and small, twinkling gems of all kind gleamed in the afternoon sunshine. "Here."

Rose pursed her lips. "You're not going to buy me a present, are you?"

"No," he said. "But that could be a pretense while I ask the lady some questions."

He could see Rose calculate a mental estimation of the shopkeeper. This one was a woman who had a large wart on her face, right between her eyes, and long, scruffy hair.

"Why do you want to ask her questions?" Rose asked.

"Because she has a pixie with her."

Rose glanced behind the voluminous folds of the woman's dress, trying not to notice how tightly the fabric was stretched across her impressive girth. Sitting down beside her, with wide, tired eyes, was another woodland pixie in a tattered dress.

"That one reminds me of the other pixie we came across in the Wandering Caverns," Rose whispered. "Bachas, right?"

"Exactly. I want to find out some information about the pixies, if we can. I'd also like to see if there is something they can do for Bachas. He has been very melancholy, and he told Ethan and Sophia this morning his leg is still bothering him."

"We can ask Philip if there's anything at the palace for him," Rose said. "I know Mary has said he is nothing but rude to her."

"Maybe if he feels better, he'll be easier to deal with," Theo suggested.

Rose relented at his reasoning, and the two of them made their way to the stand. The lady blinked up at them and brushed her hair out of her eyes, letting Theo and Rose have a much clearer view of the wart. It wiggled in greeting as they watched her.

"What's your pleasure?" the lady asked, her voice as scraggly as her gown was tattered. "I am Madame Sageberry. Welcome to my shop."

"I have heard about pixie magic," Theo began inconspicuously, "and I wanted to see what kind of gems you had for sale here."

The woman's eyes lit up with a mercenary gleam. "I have plenty for sale. What kind of magic do you need? Protection from magic? Need to ward off fairies?"

"Do they actually work?" Rose asked. She glanced over at the pixie, who cowed at her look.

"Of course they do. Nothing but the best from Madame Sageberry."

"I'm looking for some healing magic," Theo said. "It's for a pixie with a pained leg."

"A special order." Madame Sageberry grinned, showing off her brittle teeth. "Excellent. Mora, get to work." She turned to the little pixie, who nodded and took a gem down from a nearby table. As she held it, the gem began to glow in different colors.

"Is this your pixie?" Rose asked. "She's beautiful."

The pixie looked up at her with a tepid smile, even though Theo thought he saw her tremble.

"Bah, there's no need to flatter her," Madame Sageberry snapped as Mora handed her the newly-minted gem. "She's bound to me by a life debt. She'll do the spell and the magic so it will work perfectly, or she'll be punished."

"There's no need for that," Theo said, as he handed off some coins to Madame Sageberry. She handed him the gem in return, and he quickly pocketed it.

"I agree. But if you have any trouble with the order, you can bet I'll hear about it and punish her for it."

The pixie nodded dutifully up at Rose, who suddenly had a determined look on her face. "How much for the pixie?" she asked.

Madame Sageberry scoffed at her. "You can't transfer a life debt," she said. "Mora here is mine until I die."

"Can't you set her free?" Rose asked. "I have plenty of money. We would be happy to compensate you for her."

"We don't have that much," Theo whispered softly.

"Theo," Rose murmured back. "We have to do something."

Before Theo could reply, Madame Sageberry drew herself up proudly. "I'll not be bought," she declared. "I saved this pixie's life, and it is her duty to serve me for the rest of mine. Now, take yourselves off before I charge you more."

"But—"

Madame Sageberry took a menacing step closer to Mora, who gave the barest hint of a flinch. "Don't bring more trouble to poor Mora, here, lady. I'd hate to punish her for your insolence."

"My insolence?" Rose huffed. "What about yours?"

Seeing that Mora was in danger of getting attacked by her mistress, Theo stepped in. "Thank you for your help today," he said, doing his best to keep his tone civil.

"Theo," Rose grumbled. "No."

"Rose." Theo tugged on her arm gently. "Come on."

"Be on your way!" Madame Sageberry hollered. "I'd hate to call the kingdom guards."

Theo stopped Rose from telling Madame Sageberry to go ahead and do just that by pulling her hand and leading her down the street. Theo managed to duck into a small alcove by a side street when Rose managed to free herself from his grip.

"What do you think you're doing?" Rose snarled. "She was abusing that pixie."

"And by the pixie's own laws, there's nothing to be done about it," Theo reminded her. "At least, nothing short of killing Madame Sageberry."

"Don't tempt me."

"That's exactly why I was trying to get you to leave," he told her. "This isn't Rhone. We're here for Isra, and at Philip and his family's pleasure. There wasn't anything we could do for Mora, and this isn't something where we can get involved in the kingdom politics. The pixies have their own governing rules."

"It's just so unfair," Rose said. She put her head in her hands, angry and sad.

"I know." He pulled her close, wrapping his arms around her while she put her head on his chest. Theo sensed she was not just thinking of Mora's fate, but her own as well.

Moments passed before Rose eased back from him. "I'm sorry," she muttered. "If I stand around here and mope at all the awful things in the world, I'll never do anything else."

"It's alright. I know how you feel about things like this," Theo told her. "And it's nice you still mourn for it. More cynical people would dismiss it. You bring beauty to the world, Rose, even when you cry over its ugliness."

"I know I can't solve every problem, but it makes me miserable to see other people in the same situation as I am."

"Mora's mistress seems old," Theo said, trying to find a way to comfort her. "Maybe it won't be too long before she's free."

Rose shrugged. "It's shameful she has to be bound to her in the first place."

"Bachas would probably agree," Theo said, thinking of the small pixie rooming with Sophia and Mary. He recalled the glorious joy on Bachas' face, as he realized he was no longer bound to serve his master. "I know that made you unhappy. Let's hope this gemstone we bought will heal him, so some good will come out of this."

Rose nodded. "I hope it helps."

"I know you're not used being unable to do something when it comes to tough situations like this."

Rose snorted. "That's my whole life."

"Even with just Magdalina's curse, you have done everything but nothing." Theo gave her a kind smile. "Just watch. You'll be able to overcome her yet."

He felt her tense. "Even with the dragon's blood," she said, "I'll have to find a way to fight her."

"*We* will find a way to fight her, Rose," he corrected her. "Magdalina does not have many friends the way you do."

"She still has magic she can use."

Theo dropped his hand into hers. "There are things besides magic we have at our disposal. We'll use it all to find a way to free you," he said, catching her eyes with his. "I promise you, Rosary."

Rose finally managed a smile. "I guess you'll just have to say your prayers, huh?"

At the subtle scorn in her voice, Theo sighed. "Later," he said. "For now, I'll settle for getting you that food you wanted."

"I don't know if I have an appetite anymore."

"I can't blame you for that," Theo agreed. "Still, let's keep moving. Maybe we'll find something else."

As they made their way through the town, Theo turned his thoughts to what Enrique had said earlier about his aunt.

His mother's sister was still alive. Why had he not been told? He barely remembered her at all; she had sent gifts for Christmas one year. Surely his grandfather would have let him know that his other daughter was still alive.

But then, Theo knew, the old reverend never seemed to share much with him, or even Thad, in all the years they had lived under the protection of the church.

ONCE UPON A PRINCESS

14

Rose sighed as she stared out the window of her room, watching as a parade of servants and guards all shuffled through the palace, putting the final touches on the palace as guests began to arrive for Philip and Isra's engagement ball. Part of her was keeping an ear out for Ambassador Rolez's name as announcements were made, but most of her mind was content to linger elsewhere.

"Enjoying the view?" Mary asked.

Rose glanced up to see Mary as she appeared inside her room. "Not really," Rose admitted. "This makes me think too much of my last birthday party." She grimaced at her accidental choice of words.

Mary came up to her. "You're not the only one who is down," she said. "I was finally able to sneak away from Bachas. Fiona's taking a turn helping your squire and her brother watch him."

"I take it he hasn't been any less obnoxious since Theo brought back that healing gem for him?"

"Not to me," Mary replied. "He's warmed up to Theo considerably, though."

Rose felt a small smile curl on her lips. "That's not hard to believe."

"Okay, I'm just going to say it." Mary sighed. "You know, you really should just tell Theo what Magdalina said to you. He asked me about it. He hasn't forgotten about it."

"Neither have I," Rose said curtly. "He's just been playing the waiting game, hasn't he?"

"As much as I'm surprised by it myself, I would say no. He's got something else on his mind. He has been distracted ever since you came back from your unofficial tour of O'Lin."

Rose frowned. "I wonder what he's worried about."

She thought of their time in town and around the castle. Between the meals where she often had Utopa in tears, the adventures in finding Ambassador Rolez, and the distractions that came along with Isra's party, Rose realized she had been distracted enough that she had failed to notice there was something on Theo's mind.

"What is he doing now?" she asked Mary.

"He and Ronan are playing a game of chess in one of the palace dens," Mary said. "But as more guests arrive, I imagine he'll meet us outside in the ballroom."

"I guess that's good. Let's hope he remains distracted, so he will forget about me and my secrets."

"I don't know why you don't just tell him and the others about Magdalina's deal."

"Because I don't need any more pity," Rose explained. "I love my friends, Mary. You are all so special to me. But I know you all worry for me, and you're all here for me. I can't ask anything else of you."

"Rose, you have always been so fiercely independent," Mary said. "I fear too much at times. We all need help at times. And you know we are all here willingly."

"That makes it worse," Rose argued. "If it were something I could pay for, I would pay for it in a heartbeat. Then I wouldn't have to worry about letting all of my friends down in addition to my kingdom."

Mary shook her head, making her wings shimmer. "Please, Rose—"

Rose shook her head. "It's too hard for me to explain, Mary."

"It's not for me," Mary said. "You're too proud, Rose, and you're too afraid and angry."

"So?" Rose crossed her arms and looked down at the scene outside once more. "Don't I have a right to that?"

"You might not be able to stop how you feel, but you can choose how you respond to it. And that includes trusting us and having faith that we can make a difference together."

Mary cleared her throat. "You know, Magdalina is in a similar situation. She doesn't trust anyone, Rose. She has no friends, except for maybe Everon. All of her supporters have other, more personal or selfish reasons for serving her."

"What are you saying?" Rose asked. "That I'm just like her?"

"Don't twist my words, Rose," Mary chided. "I'm saying you can make different choices than what she's made, and you should. Especially if you want to beat her."

Rose went quiet once more. Theo had said something similar earlier; he had been adamant that they would defeat her together.

"Please, think about it," Mary said. "I'm going to go and help Isra get ready now. I'll see you downstairs soon, right?"

Rose only nodded, her gaze firm as she continued to watch as new guests arrived.

She waited until she was certain Mary was gone, and then she heaved a heavy sigh. As much as she hated to admit it, Mary had a good point. She let her fingers tangle around the prayer beads Theo had given her.

Rose hated how much both Mary and Theo were right. She knew, despite her fear, and in spite of her anger, she could trust them. She had no reason to doubt them with her secrets. They had both been with her since the beginning.

ONCE UPON A PRINCESS

Technically even before then, too. Rose rolled the rosary beads between her fingers, shocked to realize it had been over ten years since she had first met Theo.

He had been so precious, she thought, that first time she had seen him.

Devastated to realize she was pitied, rather than beloved by her nation, Rose had run to the comfort of the church, which she had always loved for its grand design and inspiring artwork.

She had come to cry at the altar, only to find a precocious altar boy cleaning as she came rushing in. He had been stubborn and matter of fact about the matter, telling her of Magdalina and her curse. He did not even realize she was the princess as he told her the truth; when she told him that she was, he told her, laughingly, that she couldn't be Princess Aurora, because the Princess of Rhone was supposed to be beautiful and kind.

She had punched him for that, causing his nose to bleed all over his wrinkled robes.

Rose smiled as she recalled that feeling of power. There was something inside of her, she'd realized, that could fight. She had been so shocked she did not even think about the boy until later. She decided she would keep him around her to remind her that she had the power inside of her to overcome her troubles.

Later, she thought, she had come to rely on him for much more than that.

Before Rose could sink further into her thoughts, she heard another announcement.

"Ambassador Alfonse Rolez!"

Rose peeked out the window. She watched as the ambassador, a short man, dressed in glided robes and tall boots, as he made his way through the receiving line.

"He's here!" Rose cheered. She knew she had a lot of problems to solve and decisions to make; this was likely her only chance to get to talk with the ambassador. Enrique had been right; he had closed his house off to all visitors, and if the snooty look on his high-mustached, tight-lipped expression was any indication, Rose had a feeling he was only attending the ball tonight at the compulsion of Utopa. She was going to make sure she took full advantage of his appearance.

She headed downstairs at once.

"Check."

Theo grimaced, aware he had been unable to concentrate on the game in front of him. He glanced up at Rose's younger brother, Ronan, with a look of tired sadness.

"Come on," Ronan insisted. "This is war. No sympathies, Theo."

Ronan, as Isra's twin, was just over sixteen, but in many ways, he seemed much younger than Isra, and especially much younger than Rose. He loved to play games, to go hunting and fishing, and he never had enough adventure. Theo was convinced that King Stefanos had sent him out on his Grand Tour of Rhone just to get him away from the castle at Havilah.

Theo chuckled. "It's still worth a try, isn't it?" he asked, as he moved his king out of danger. "Besides, it'll make the game last longer."

"Ha." Ronan smirked. "I can see why Rose is always warning me not to get into an argument with you. You're very convincing. Check."

"Not convincing enough, obviously," Theo said, "since you're still intent on defeating me." He moved his king once more, shuffling him toward the middle of the playing field, already feeling defeat.

"Checkmate!" Ronan jumped up and cheered, slamming his knight down on its final square. "Woo-hoo!"

Theo grinned. "Alright, you won," he said. "There's no need to make me feel old in addition to feeling vanquished."

Ronan continued to celebrate, and Theo eventually laughed. Ronan was still young, but even with taking his age into account, he seemed much happier than his father.

"Come on," Theo said, after another moment. "Didn't your father ever teach you to win with dignity?"

Ronan quickly sobered at the mention of the King. "When has my father done anything with dignity?" he asked. "You have not been around as much as I have in the last five years, Theo. The King is a mess."

"I know he's getting older," Theo said. "But from what I have seen, he seems to be keeping the kingdom together."

"Barely." Ronan sat back down. "That was part of the reason he sent for Rose, you know. He was content to groom me and Isra for the crown until the rumors about Magdalina started."

"What rumors?"

"She's been hanging around the castle at Havilah more," Ronan said. "Or at least, that's what he says. I talked with his physician a few times. I think he's going mad."

"Rose is having a hard time with her curse, too," Theo said, trying to keep his voice even.

"He's not worried about her. He's worried about himself." Ronan shook his head. "There's always more talk about what will happen if Rose does succumb to her curse. A lot of people are scared for her."

"Well, they're scared for themselves," Theo said. "I don't think any of them actually care too much about what she's had to go through."

"True, true." Ronan nodded. "But the King still hasn't told the majority of the country that he has Isra and me to fall back on. And then he went and imprisoned our mother? If it's one thing I saw on my trip, Theo, it's that people are angry and scared, and they're losing faith in the king."

"What do you think?"

"I think," Ronan said, "I'm going to enjoy watching Rose when she gets back. She's going to have a bit of a tangle to unravel. But even in the three days she was home, she managed to inspire plenty of our citizens. I think just getting her back there and back to work will make a lot of people much happier. I heard about her visit all the way across the country."

Theo was just about to ask him about Magdalina again when Rose entered the room.

"And there she is," Ronan said, jumping up. "I was just talking about you, Rose."

Rose scowled at Theo. "Why?" she asked.

Theo shrugged before he realized that she was probably worried he was telling Ronan about their serendipitous meeting at the hot springs.

"I was just commenting on how the King seems to be having a hard time," Ronan said. "When I passed through Rhone on my Grand Tour, there were plenty who were already worried enough. Now we have the Queen to worry about."

"How has she been?" Rose asked. "Did you hear anything from her lately?"

"She's fine. Virtue came with a pack of letters earlier today," Ronan told her.

"Virtue's here?" Rose grinned. "Wonderful! I will have to go and see him after we're finished with business tonight."

"I guess it is time to go," Theo said, standing up.

"Yes, it is," Rose agreed. "I saw the ambassador arrive. He's here. We need to make sure we can interview him before he leaves."

Ronan forced a yawn. "I guess that's my cue to go and give my proper greeting to Philip and Isra, before I sneak out and find more interesting things to do."

"More interesting things to do?" Rose repeated.

Ronan gave her a smirk. "Come on, Rose," he said. "You have to admit, town life is a lot more lively than the palace."

"You're going to go to the town and party?" Rose wrinkled her nose in disapproval. "Ronan."

"Get over it, Rose," Ronan said. "I'm going to be stuck in palaces all my life. Let me have some fun."

"You'd better not get into any trouble, or that palace will easily become your prison."

"It's not like it hasn't been before," Ronan scoffed. He turned to Theo. "Hey, you want to come with me? I could use someone with an honest face, especially when things get really wild."

"He's not going with you," Rose snapped.

"Let the man decide for himself, Rose," Ronan replied. "And lighten up. It's not like I don't like Philip. He's a nice guy. But I don't want to stay here and watch him stare at Isra all night. And you and Theo have your mysteries to solve and stuff to do. All I have to do is make nice with the people, and I can score better points here by hanging out with the locals."

Theo stepped in. "I'm going to stay with Rose," he said. "We'll see you down in the main hall."

Ronan grinned and waved as he stepped out of the room.

Rose huffed. "That brother of mine."

"He used to do the same thing when we were in Rhone," Theo said. "I remember him going out as early as twelve, Rose."

Rose shook her head. "Still," she said, "he doesn't seem to take anything seriously."

"That's why Isra was born before him," Theo joked. He cleared his throat. "In all seriousness, though, he's a good kid, Rose. But he's still a kid. And Roderick and Lannister are also ready to watch him for us."

Rose gave him a small smile. "I should have known there were contingency plans," she said. "And did you say Lannister was back from King Derick?"

"Yes, he is," Theo said. "The traders have been picked up and the rest of the caverns have been cleared. Lannister has an official report for you, but I left it upstairs with the mail."

"Good." Rose nodded. "This is a good night for news. Let's hope the honorable Ambassador Alfonse Rolez will give us some more." She put on a dazzling smile as she reached for his arm once more.

"Remember your promise."

"Promise? What promise?"

"No charm this time," Theo said with a smile. "Intimidation only."

Rose laughed as they headed down to meet with Isra and her guests.

15

Rose clutched onto Theo's arm more tightly as they maneuvered their way closer to where the ambassador was standing. There were people dancing and chatting in circles of friends, all while servants were ducking and sliding around them and each other.

She allowed herself a moment to take in the scene around her. The servants had cleaned up the room since they had arrived, and the room sparkled—although Rose had a feeling that was more due to Mary and Juana's magic at work. The music swelled as Theo guided her past the music pit.

At the front of the room, Rose could see Isra and Philip as they stood together, greeting their guests in small groups.

"Isra looks beautiful," Theo said, as they drifted along with the crowd.

"She has always been beautiful," Rose said. She watched as Isra took a step closer to Philip, who towered over her. She watched as he leaned down to hear Isra as she said something to him.

"They really do seem to like each other."

"She's so young," Rose said. "I worry for her."

"Philip's our friend," Theo said. "And they do have a lot in common."

"That doesn't mean much." Rose watched Philip take hold of Isra's hand, interlacing his fingers with hers.

"Of course you would think so," Theo said.

"What's that supposed to mean?" Rose snapped. "I'm not against their relationship, but there's nothing wrong with thinking things through carefully."

"I know that, and I agree with that," Theo replied, this time with some hesitation in his voice. "But you have to admit, you don't like to trust in things that you can't see or touch or prove."

Rose glared at him. Before she could roundly dismiss him, she caught a glimpse of shining gold out of the corner of her eye.

Theo followed her gaze. "That's the ambassador?"

Rose watched as the man she had seen earlier took a glass of wine from one of the servants. "Yes," Rose answered. "I'm certain that it's him."

Theo glanced around. "We should see if we can get him to go into another room," he said.

"There's a corridor leading to the kitchens over that way." Rose pulled him after her, as they hurried as politely and non-chalantly as possible through the crowd once more, this time with a destination in sight. "What do you think?"

"That will work."

Rose felt a rush of excitement as they slipped around to where the ambassador was standing. Their movements were coordinated over the past years of battles and sparring, and Rose knew they would get their prize.

Theo came up from Ambassador Rolez's right side, while she slipped in front of him.

"Ambassador," she said in greeting. "How very nice to make your acquaintance."

The man drew himself up proudly, flinching as Theo came into view. "I say, what do you think you're doing?" he sputtered.

"We would like to ask you a few questions," Rose said. "And this is exactly as charming as I'm going to be."

"Hmmph. Well, you don't appeal to me in the least," the man said. "I'd recognize you anywhere."

"That's right," Rose said, rolling her eyes. "I'm Princess Aurora of Rhone."

"I hardly need an introduction, Your Highness." Rolez narrowed his shifty eyes at her. "One doesn't even have to look closely to see you and your uncle have a similar cunning aspect to your face."

"My uncle?" Rose repeated. "That's a new one. Most people cite the beauty or the grace or something else when they recognize me."

"How do you know Rose's uncle?" Theo asked.

"Oh, you're going to ask questions, too, are you?" Rolez's face began to turn purple. "I think I've had enough of this conversation. Excuse me."

"Stop," Rose commanded. "We want to talk to you."

"Well, *I* don't want to talk to *you*."

"*You* don't want to make *us* mad," Rose insisted. "This is my sister's engagement party, remember? We just want some answers, and then we'll be on our way, and you don't have to deal with us again."

"Good. I wouldn't want to deal with anyone from Hebert's family. The man might have been my brother-in-law, but if I had my way, I would take him to court even *after* my sister's death just to get them divorced."

"So your sister was married to my uncle," Rose realized.

"We are sorry for your loss," Theo chimed in quickly.

"You should be," Rolez muttered. "All those years, and she has been absolutely miserable."

Rose thought about what Enrique said. "At least you were there for her," she said quietly. "You were able to make it better for her."

"For all the good it did in the end," Rolez muttered. "She had the best doctors looking after her. But she died because your uncle was horrible to her."

"What did he do?" Rose asked, appalled by the thought.

"He neglected her," Rolez snapped. "She wanted children and a family, and he locked her out of his side of their house in Aragon. She was cast away every day they were married."

"Why?"

"Why do you think?" Rolez scoffed. "He was in love with someone else. I don't know who, and neither did my beloved Isabel, but she knew. How could a wife not know when she is not wanted?"

Rolez teared up and pulled out a handkerchief. "See? See what you've made me do now? I'm going to be all flummoxed for this entire affair now."

"I'm sorry for your loss, sir," Rose said, trying to be kinder. She patted his arm gently, barely touching him. He slid away from her as she advanced, but Theo held him close. "But we still have to ask you some questions. Where did you buy that tapestry? The one you gave to Queen Juliette?"

Rolez's despair vanished as proud defiance took its place. "I'd forgotten about that!" he said. "Why do you want to know? It's not my fault if she's in danger."

Rose and Theo exchanged concerned glances.

Seeming to sense his mistake, Rolez waved it away. "Never mind about it. The tapestry was just a gift."

A quiet voice spoke up from behind them. "He's lying."

Rose and Theo whirled around to see Bachas as he came up the hall from behind them.

"Bachas," Theo said. "What are you doing here? You should be resting. Your leg—"

"Is much better now, thank you very much."

152

Rose knew from Theo's expression he was just as shocked as she was by the genuine politeness in his tone.

"It's so good," Bachas said, "that I can now use my own magic."

Rose tensed. *Where are Mary and Fiona? Is he going to attack us?*

"Which means, Ambassador, you might want to think again before running off."

A snap crackled between them, and Rolez was suddenly whimpering. He was frozen in a half-jump, caught between sprints.

"What are you doing here?" Theo asked.

"I thought about your offer," Bachas said. "And I've decided to help you—if you'll help me in return."

"I will do what I can to help you if you need it," Theo said. "But I want specifics before entering into a deal with you."

"Later," Bachas said. "Right now, we need to get this guy to tell us where Annalora is."

Rolez struggled even harder. "I'm going to scream!" he yelled, before there was another snap of power, and his voice went mute.

"Scream all you like," Bachas muttered, as he guided Rolez's frozen, mid-air body further into the darkness of the hall. "In fact, I welcome it, if that means I'll be able to keep you from blubbering."

"I'm not sure of this," Rose whispered to Theo.

"Me, either," he admitted. "I know he was really happy to get the healing stone from me earlier, but I didn't think it would make him violent."

"Where's Mary or Fiona when you need them?" Rose asked.

"Probably with Isra," he said. "They are serving as the official chaperones tonight."

"Oh, I forgot about that," Rose admitted.

Behind them, Bachas allowed Rolez to regain his voice, and Rolez was clearly not happy about the situation.

"Let me go," he said. "Or I'll have charges taken up against you."

"I can make you forget everything with a snap of my fingers," Bachas told him. "So I'm not worried about you at all."

"Bachas," Theo said. "Maybe we can ease up a little?"

"Only after he tells us where we can find Annalora," Bachas said. He rounded on Rolez. "Tell us!"

"Okay," he muttered. "I ordered a tapestry from her for the new queen."

"Why do you think Queen Juliette is in danger?" Rose asked.

"Because he knows Annalora makes the tapestries with Magdust," Bachas told her. "He went to go and meet with her precisely because of that."

"How do you know?" Theo asked.

"I know," Bachas snapped.

Rolez squirmed. "Fine. The pixie's right," he admitted. "I didn't want anything bad to happen to her or the King, per say. I just wanted to punish Rhone."

"So you endangered the lives of Einish's monarchs?" Rose asked. "Why?"

"Tell us." Theo's voice went dark and hard. "If she's in danger, you will tell us now."

"Did you think the Queen was in danger because of the Magdust?" Rose asked.

"Magdust in small doses is gradually supposed to affect people," Rolez muttered. "I didn't think anyone would notice. It hasn't been that long since she received it from me."

"What was the tapestry for?" Rose repeated.

ONCE UPON A PRINCESS

When he did not answer, she grabbed Rolez by the ear and dragged him further down into the darkened alcove.

"Nothing," he shouted. "Nothing I swear!"

"That's a lie. Tell us!"

"Allow me to help with the persuasion," Bachas said, snapping his fingers. Rolez dropped to the floor from his frozen state. The diplomat easily crumbled over into a ball.

"Alright, fine," Rolez snapped. "But stop it. I'm not cut out for this. Or starting a war, apparently."

"You wanted to start a war?" Rose gave him a skeptical look. "How would that work?"

"Once it became known that the Queen of Einish had a special Magdust tapestry, the fairies would revolt, and Rhone would be upset with her for encouraging the enterprise that has weakened their whole national community," Rolez said. "The engagement between the Princess of Rhone and the Prince of Einish would be cancelled, and Crystal Lake would be weakened further by its inability to gain support. The people would be ripe for a rebellion."

Rose and Theo exchanged a quick glance. "Maybe we should get him to a guard," she said. "It sounds like there's enough there to get him arrested."

"I was just thinking the same thing," Theo said with a nod.

"No!" Bachas jumped up again. "No, he's not going anywhere, until he tells us how to find Annalora."

"Right." Rose turned to him. "Where can we find Annalora?"

Rolez looked terrified. "You aren't going to tell her I told you, are you? She knows how to get revenge on people."

"We won't tell her," Rose said, but Bachas interrupted her.

ONCE UPON A PRINCESS

"If you don't tell us where to find her, you won't have to worry about her coming for revenge," he said. "I'll take care of it myself."

Rose nearly choked. "Come on, Bachas," she said. "There's no need to put that kind of pressure on him."

"I'm a free pixie," he scoffed. "I'll do what I want."

"Bachas," Theo started to say, as Bachas snapped his fingers once more.

Rolez cried out in pain. "No!"

"Stop it," Rose insisted.

"Not until he agrees to tell us!" Bachas shouted back.

"Fine, fine," Rolez cried out. "I'll tell you. Just let me go."

Bachas folded his hands, and the flow of power halted.

"Annalora only takes on special commissions," Rolez said. "I heard about her and her tapestries as a child. I didn't think they were real. But when I was passing through Rhone, there was a tournament. She was there, trying to sell her work. When she caught sight of me, she approached me and began talking to me."

"She found you?" Theo asked.

"Yes. She told me she would have a tapestry ready for me by the time I went back to Einish with my sister. I was picking up Isabel from her manor, and taking her back with me. She had written to me, telling me that Hebert had been raging with her and arguing with her more often lately. She never stays home for long while he is there, but it was especially bad, so I went to go and secure her myself."

"I'm sorry for your sister's trouble," Rose said. "I don't know my uncle, but I can assure you he is nothing like me."

"I don't care," Rolez spat. "You're still his blood."

"But I'm not him!" Rose argued.

"I don't care," Bachas said. "How did you find the tournament?"

"It was close to the Aragonian border, about a week's ride from Havilah," he said. "You follow the main trail to Aragon, and close to the border, there is a place where tournaments are held. Annalora lives close by, on the outskirts of a town called Urra."

"Urra," Theo repeated. "I've never heard of it."

"That's where she lives." Rolez nodded to Bachas. "You can even use your magic to see I am telling the truth."

Bachas did not stop to question him. He simply grabbed Rolez's hand. A moment later, as a light poured out from their hands, Bachas nodded. "I believe you."

"Can I go now?" Rolez groaned. "I don't want to be here any longer."

"Be gone!" Bachas clapped his hands, and Rolez disappeared.

Rose frowned. "I'm glad to see you're feeling better, but he had just confessed to ordering that tapestry for the Queen in order to start a trade war. I would have preferred to have Philip question him."

"Your friend can question him later," Bachas said. "I sent him to a cell in the dungeon here."

"We thank you for your consideration." Theo knelt down beside the small pixie. "And for your help in getting the information. But I have to wonder, why are you so concerned with our mission?"

"I need to know where Annalora is," Bachas said. "She's using pixie magic to hide herself from my seeing stone." He pulled out a small marble from his pocket and handed it to Theo.

As Rose and Theo examined the small gemstone, it glowed with power, and a small, feminine pixie face came into its center.

"My beloved wife, Elva," Bachas explained. "Once I was bound in a life debt, I was unable to use my magic for anything except what my master said. Now I can see her again, and she is also in a life debt."

"To Annalora," Rose guessed.

Bachas nodded. "I have to go and free her. I know you are looking for Annalora too. I will need your help in finding her, so I can see Elva again."

"I don't know how we can help," Rose told him. "Annalora is a concern for us, but it is one we will have to address after we have dealt with Magdalina. But maybe King Derick will be able to help you. He is the one who should be the most upset at the issue with the tapestry, especially since it was given to Juliette."

"That won't work," Bachas said. He pointed at Theo. "He's the one who can get me back to Elva."

"Why's that?" Rose asked. "You already told him that he's not a priest, so he doesn't have the protection from your magic that they do."

"He's—"

Theo stepped forward and cut him off. "She's my aunt," he admitted quietly. "Annalora is my mother's sister."

Rose felt her mouth drop open in surprise.

16

The surprise on Rose's face was immediately washed away and replaced with suspicion. "Why didn't you tell me?" she asked Theo.

He watched her eyes narrow, and he suddenly felt irritated. He was entitled to his secrets, same as she was, and he told her so. "We all have secrets, Rose."

Instantly, Rose crossed her arms over her chest and prepared for battle.

He inwardly groaned. He did not want to fight her, especially now, when they were supposed to be having a good time, celebrating Isra's engagement.

"You still should have told me," Rose insisted.

"We have enough to do as it is," Theo replied. "You just said it yourself: Magdalina is our first priority."

"That doesn't mean that we just push everything off to the side," Rose said. "Especially when we're face to face with the issue like we are right now."

Bachas cleared his throat. "I think I'm going to take my leave," he said. "My leg is better, but still sore, and I don't think I want to get caught in the middle of a fight."

"We are not fighting," Rose snapped down at him.

Bachas smirked slyly. "Call it what you want, Princess," he said. "But I'm not stupid."

Before she could correct him, he snapped his fingers and disappeared.

"We are not fighting," Rose repeated, as if saying it again would make her believe it more.

"I don't want to fight you," Theo told her. "But you are keeping secrets from me, too, and if I'm forced to tell you mine, I want to hear yours."

"You don't want to know my secrets," Rose told him, her voice suddenly so weary Theo almost wondered if he should sit her down somewhere.

Maybe I should leave her alone. This has been a long day, and we will be heading back to Rhone soon.

He decided to go. He did not want to have to tell her about his family history, and it was easier just to leave. "Excuse me," he said, before heading down the hall.

Theo was not surprised when she started following him. "Where are you going?" Rose asked, as she followed him. "We're not finished talking."

"I don't want to talk to you right now," he told her.

"Why?"

"I already told you." He pushed open a door at the end of the hall and found himself outside, on a small balcony overlooking the gardens. "I don't want to talk about Annalora, any more than you want to talk about what's bothering you."

Rose grabbed his arm and stepped in front of him. "Don't you trust me?"

Theo stopped. "That's an unfair question, Rose," he said.

"Why?" Rose put her hands on her hips.

"Because I know you were lying when I talked to you in the caverns," he said.

"I'm just trying to protect you," Rose snapped.

"I don't want your protection," Theo argued. "I want the truth."

"There's no need to get angry about it."

"If that were true, why do you need to know about my family?" Theo asked.

"Are you worried I would judge you because of them?" Rose asked. "Because you know I wouldn't. You have never done that to me, even though the King has never warmed up to you."

"No," Theo said. "You know I don't talk about them much, and that's because I don't know a lot about them myself. When Enrique told me about my mother's death, I didn't know what to say."

"There isn't much you can say," Rose told him, as she stepped up beside him.

"It's still a shock," Theo told her. He made his way over to the edge of the balcony and gripped its wall. "After Thad told me he'd found my uncle's letter to our grandfather, and I learned more about them, I knew there were connections to the Magdust trade. But I never imagined it would go this far. I don't want to talk about it."

"According to Bachas," Rose said, "Annalora is using Elva's magic to protect herself. You might be the only one who can really help him, since you're related to her."

"I don't know what good that will do," Theo said. "My mother and father still died."

"By Everon's hand," Rose reminded him gently. "Not Annalora's."

"I guess so." Theo shrugged. "You know, I never thought about it much, but this is part of the reason Jesus said not to judge. I can't help but wonder if my parents deserved to die, for participating in the Magdust trade as they did. Especially after hearing all of this."

"You're the one who would tell me that we're all fallen," Rose said as she came up beside him. "You would also tell me that good things can still come from bad things."

ONCE UPON A PRINCESS

Theo gave her a sad smile. "Is this your revenge for when I try to comfort you?"

"Maybe," she teased. "But not really. It's true, isn't it? If nothing had happened to your parents, I never would have met you."

"Just like if you hadn't been cursed, we might have never become friends." Theo sighed. "And I would have had to watch you grow up with all those suitors around, watching them fall over themselves as they charmed you, and you would have been charmed by them."

Rose made a face. "I would not," she insisted. "Some of them were terrible. Even without my curse, I wouldn't have liked them. They were still too focused on what I looked like, anyway."

"Are you saying that your beauty is more of a curse than the one Magdalina bestowed upon you?" Theo asked. He reached over and tugged on a lock of her hair, teasing her back. As Rose laughed, Theo found himself running his hand through her hair. It was soft and delicate and strangely enthralling.

Under the light of the moon and surrounded by the magic of night, she was more irresistible than ever.

Even when she stopped laughing, he had a hard time letting the last of her locks slip through his fingers, forcing himself to step back.

"Either way, I don't think it matters too much," Rose answered. "I know you're worried about your family, and wondering about them, too. But it's just like everything else we face. We'll work it out." Rose laid her head against his shoulder. "Together."

Theo let her comfort him for a long moment. "Do you really believe that?" he asked.

"I do." Rose nodded.

"Then why don't you tell me what happened in the caverns?" he asked.

Rose jerked away from him. "You just had to ruin it, didn't you?"

"Ruin what?" he asked, keeping his voice innocent.

"How nice it was, being out here, with you," Rose shot back. She pushed back her hair, and he thought he saw her blush. "I mean, it could've been so nice. I comfort you, we feel better, and then we go back into the ballroom, have a nice evening, and then everything's fine. But no, you had to bring up Magdalina."

"I didn't bring her up," Theo said. "Not exactly. I just wanted to know what happened in the cave—" He stopped as he realized what she said. "That's what happened. You saw her."

Rose turned away from him, crossing her arms.

"That's it," he said again. "You saw her, and you couldn't defeat her."

"There's no need to rub it in my face!" Rose yelled.

"What did she say?" Theo asked. "Tell me, Rose."

"She told me she would take off the curse," Rose said.

For a moment, he was only full of hope and happiness. But then Theo remembered the anger and sadness in Rose's eyes as she came back to them, following the attack by the traders in the Wandering Caverns. "But she didn't, did she?"

"She said she would."

Theo walked around and stood in front of Rose. "If you did what?" he pressed.

Rose sighed. "If I married her son and made him the next King of Rhone."

Theo did not know if he was more shocked or outraged by the thought of Rose marrying Everon. Either way, he was too distracted by Rose's further silence to decide properly.

"What did you tell her?" he asked.

"I told her I was tired of people wanting to marry me," Rose said.

He felt his breath leave him in a rush.

"She had some nerve to try to convince me it was a compliment of sorts, but I didn't believe her. She told me I had until my birthday to decide."

"But you told her no, right?"

"I tried to tell her no," Rose replied.

"Rose."

"Theo," she muttered back. "Come on. You don't know what it's like. When I hear things like what Rolez just told us, about how the Magdust trade has ruined my country's hope, then I worry. I want to know that everything will work out the way I want, but there's no guarantee."

"You're saying that you would marry Everon, in order to save yourself?"

"Myself *and* my kingdom," Rose insisted. "But only if that was the only way. And I mean, *only*."

"And you actually believe Magdalina will fulfill her promise?"

"Well, it's already something I don't want to worry about," Rose said. "So I haven't really thought about it much. But I guess you're right. I don't trust her, either."

Theo shook his head. "I can't believe you," he said.

"I thought you would be more upset that I didn't manage to kill her," Rose admitted.

"No," Theo snapped. "No, I'm angry you didn't tell me about her deal, and I'm angry you didn't think it mattered enough to tell me, and then I'm angry you're not ruling it out entirely."

Rose huffed. "Well, can you blame me? My birthday is almost here, Theo. I only have four months left."

"Still, it's—"

"It's what?"

"It's not supposed to work that way between us. I have been beside you, suffering as you suffer, working as you work, for more than half our lives now. I'm not like Felise or Natala or even Sophia and Ethan and Philip. I'm not someone who just passes through your life, Rose. I'm not just going to leave you."

Theo took her by the shoulders, attempting to steady himself. He realized less than a second later that touching her was the wrong thing to do.

"What are you saying?" Rose asked. She seemed to sense the change between them at the same time. Her hands gripped onto his arms as her eyes found his.

"I'm saying there shouldn't be any secrets between us," he said, as he found himself under the spell of the moonlight once more, too swept up in the scent of the gardens, the warmth of the palace, the echo of music in the air.

"Theo?" His name came out as a whisper.

His eyes slipped down to her lips, and he heard her breath stop. "Rose."

Theo let himself take a step closer. She was not moving away; she was only watching him, waiting on him to move. He had to tell her. He had to tell her the truth.

"Rose, I—"

"Princess?" Lannister's voice called out from behind them, and the air between them suddenly turned cold.

"Remind me to retire him," Rose murmured, as they reluctantly stepped away from each other.

Theo caught her disappointment and hid a smile. He felt a little better, knowing she was as jarred by the interruption to their interlude as he was.

"Princess?" Lannister's voice called again.

"Over here," Rose responded. She stepped out from behind Theo, heading back toward the castle.

"Oh, there you are," Lannister said. "Good. I was looking for you. And you, too, actually," he added, gesturing toward Theo.

"Is something wrong?" Theo asked.

"Your brother and the Reverend Father have arrived."

"Thad's here?" Theo's eyes widened in surprise.

"Yes. They are both looking for you and the Princess. The King heard about Isra's engagement and sent them as envoys."

"That's wonderful," Rose said with a large smile on her face. "This means that the King is in agreement to the arrangement. I can sign the papers for Isra and Philip without worrying he could object."

Theo watched as Rose gave him an uncertain glance. He turned away; the moment between them had passed. And now his brother was here, waiting for them. "Let's go see them," he said.

"Yes," Rose agreed.

Together, they followed Lannister back into the castle and headed off to meet with Thad. Theo allowed himself one last look behind him, glancing back at the magic of the night, wishing he'd had the courage to confess his love for Rose when he had the chance.

17

"Theo!" Thad's enthusiastic welcome greeted them as they stepped into a small library in the castle. He raced forward and hugged his younger brother, and Rose had to envy Thad for his open affection.

Her heart was still racing as she stood there, watching as Thad and the Reverend Thorne met with Theo, greeting him alternatively with warmth and cool reserve.

She hated that Theo was right in some ways; he was a part of her life, and she had been wrong to conceal things from him. Once she saw the look on his face when she admitted the truth—that she was bound by her life and blood to do what she could for her kingdom, and that meant considering, for at least one span of a second, agreeing to Magdalina's deal—she knew it was a waste of a second to pretend she could.

Not while she was in love with Theo.

Oh, God, what have I done now?

Rose felt her heart lurch, sending the rest of her world spiraling, as the thought leaked out of her mind and into her heart before she could stop it. She wondered that the floor did not shake beneath her feet, that there was no lightning or thunder accompanying the crumbling walls inside of her.

As she stood there, watching the three men confer with each other about their travels, Rose reeled and reveled in the realization that she was in love, and it was beyond terrifying and exhilarating.

She was only interrupted from her inner freefall when Thad turned to her and knelt before her. "Your Highness," he said, his tone humble and gracious, just as welcoming as he had been to Theo.

"Brother Thad," she heard herself respond. Her eyes blinked slowly, as she looked from him to the Reverend Father, and then to Theo. She hurried to make her mind orientated for business, but she could not stop her heart from one last flutter as she looked on Theo's face.

She cleared her throat a moment later. "Please, rise," she said. "It is good to see you again. I am especially happy to see you, since Isra and Philip's engagement can be properly celebrated."

"His Majesty the King has sent us here to celebrate the engagement," Reverend Thorne said, "but he has also sent us in order to summon you home."

"I'm already on my way," Rose said. "Rhone is our next stop."

"He needs you home. He was relieved to hear that you were close by. He sent me and Brother Thad in hopes of getting you home faster."

"What's wrong?" Rose asked. "Is the Queen Mother ill? Or has there been another attempt on his life."

"A visitor has come to Rhone," Thad said. "Your Uncle Hebert has arrived, with a small legion of troops. He has come to the castle and there is a silent coup among the servants, since your uncle is demanding the release of the Queen."

Rose groaned. "Trust my family to mess everything up," she said. "And the King needs my help in fixing everything, I suppose?"

Thad nodded. "That's what we are facing right now. He sent us here as a pretext to find you and get you to leave at once for the capital."

"I don't see why he needs my help," Rose muttered.

"Your father married into the throne," Reverend Thorne spoke up, his old and ancient voice hesitant. "As your eighteenth birthday draws near, and the Queen remains in prison, many see the King's actions as hostile to the nation."

"What about Isra? And Ronan?" Rose asked. "Surely his other heirs would put settle quite a few people's concerns."

Thad and the Reverend Father exchanged knowing glances, before Thad spoke up. "You might as well know," he said slowly, "that there are rumors circling that Isra and Ronan are illegitimate heirs."

Rose remembered what Magdalina had said before; she had called Isra and Ronan her half-siblings.

"I didn't think a lot of the kingdom even knew about Isra and Ronan," Rose said, confused and frustrated. "How would they know that they are illegitimate?"

"Because *we* know." Reverend Thorne frowned at Thad.

Rose was glad when Theo reached out and put his hand on her shoulder. Her legs went numb at the news. "What?" she asked.

"The Queen has confessed, and the church has long known of King Stefanos' impotency," Reverend Thorne said.

Rose slumped down into a chair. "I apologize," she said. "I had no idea."

"I would not confess this to you, Princess, as a man of the cloth, if the rumors were not already circulating," Revered Thorne said with a sigh. "And if my grandson here hadn't just told you."

"It's written testimony, located in some of our saved records," Thad insisted. He glanced over at Theo, and Rose had to wonder if he was letting him know he was the one who had discovered the truth. Rose knew Thad liked to read. That was how they had learned so much about the dragon's blood and the Serpent's Garden.

"Yes, that too." The Reverend gave Thad a quick, stern look.

"Well," Rose murmured, "I guess that explains some of the secrets my father told me, the kind that all kings and queens keep to themselves."

"I know this must be shocking," Thad said.

"To put it mildly," Rose assured him, giving him a kind smile, before she thought of something else. "But wait," she said. "If the King was impotent, who is my father?"

"You were a miracle," Revered Thorne said. "The day the Queen told us she was pregnant with you, there was a prophecy spoken during chapel. The prophecy said you would save the crown's lineage and be a great leader. Everyone was thrilled."

"I can imagine." Rose shook her head as it all came together. Her father, knowing of his condition, went to Magdalina to see about an heir. He had agreed to her deal, that Rose would marry a fairy of Magdalina's choice. He had reneged on the deal when she was born, and that was why Magdalina had cursed her to die on her eighteenth birthday.

Her mother, grief-stricken, had flown into the arms of another man. Was it Roderick? Rose wondered, thinking of the close relationship she had witnessed between her guard and the Queen.

But he'd said he was just her friend, Rose recalled a moment later. He was her messenger to Aragon....

Where her father's brother lived, married to a woman he neglected.

Rose's eyes widened at the possibility. Was it her uncle who was Isra and Ronan's real father?

"And you said Uncle Hebert has come to rescue my mother?" Rose asked.

"Yes," Thad answered with a nod.

"I see." Rose sank back into her chair. "Did you find out who was behind the attack on the King? The one who tried to poison him?"

"No one other than the Queen has come under investigation."

Rose rubbed her temples. "Well, I guess everything is a mess at home," she said.

"We believe you are under the protection of our Lord and Savior," Reverend Thorne told her. "We are prepared to follow you, Princess. Our nation has heard of your conquests and your trials. We know you have found the dragon's lair and secured its blood."

Rose looked at Theo. She saw the concern on his face, the fire in his eyes.

"I have never found myself to be under much protection from God," Rose said slowly, "but I do think you are right. I need to go home and make things right with Rhone."

She was tempted to tell them she would go home and fix her parents' mess, but she decided it was not what the representatives to her kingdom needed to hear. "Excuse me," she said, standing up. "I need to go and get ready."

Thad and Reverend Thorne bowed their heads, but Theo reached for her.

She shook her head at him. "We'll talk later," she said. "Not now."

He seemed to sense the sadness behind her words, and said nothing. He only nodded and watched her leave.

18

Theo waited until Rose was out of the room before he turned back to face his brother and grandfather. He kept one ear out for the softening of Rose's footsteps, as he did not want her to interrupt them.

Rose had family issues of her own to contend with; Theo did not want her to get in the middle of his.

"What is it?" Reverend Thorne sighed heavily as Theo came up beside him.

"I want to know about Annalora," he said.

Theo had to give his grandfather credit; the old man only blinked at him. Thad, on the other hand, gasped in surprise. "Annalora is alive?"

"Yes," Theo said. "I have some idea of where she is located, and I would like to know more about her."

"Why?" The Reverend's eyes narrowed. "She is nothing but trouble, Theophilus, and you would do well to forget about her entirely as I have."

"I doubt you really mean that," Thad said gently.

Theo did not indulge his grandfather as Thad did. "I need to know more about her," he said, "because she has been causing trouble for Rhone and other nations now."

"What have you heard?" Reverend Thorne asked, only slightly concerned.

"She's still working in the Magdust trade, for one."

"That's no surprise," his grandfather replied. "Her mother was a talented weaver, and she taught Annalora and Eleanora everything she knew."

"I also found out with the help of a friend she's using pixie magic to cover her tracks, but she's still active in the Magdust trade. She's using her weaving talent to make enchanted tapestries, just like the one we used to have in our home."

Thad met Theo's eyes. "I remember that one. The one of Queen Lucia?"

"Yes." Theo nodded. "That's the one. She recently made another one for the new Queen of Einish."

Reverend Thorne was increasingly still. "I see."

"Is that all you have to say?" Theo asked.

"I've known about the magic for a lot longer than you have," Reverend Thorne said. "Why do you think your uncle had to write me a letter? I barely had any idea of what kind of life Eleanora had lived. It had been so many years since your grandmother had died, and I had disowned them for their sin."

"You didn't report them?" Thad asked.

"No," Reverend Thorne's pale cheeks burned red. "I did not want to get caught up in all their trouble again."

"You didn't do anything to protect other people?" Theo shook his head. "Do you know how many fairies and other people have died because of your inaction?"

"It's not like I could have saved anyone for certain." The older man's eyebrows furrowed together in grave concern. "I told you, I lost track of them years ago. I doubt I would have heard from Eleanora again if she had lived. There is no way to change the past."

"No," Theo agreed, "but we can change the future. We need to find Annalora and bring her to justice. For all the fairies she's killed and all the people whose lives she's ruined. And for Rhone. The Princess wants to stop the Magdust trade, and it's up to us to do what we can to stop her."

"We cannot do anything that will stop her," the Reverend moaned.

"I don't believe that," Theo said. "I'm more likely to believe that you just don't want to do anything."

"Well, I don't," the Reverend snapped. "Eleanora and Annalora died to me the day they decided to follow after my mother's profession. Weaving magic into fabric, all for the sake of silly wishes to be fulfilled. They didn't seem to think some that fairies would have a problem with that."

Thad frowned. "Would the love of our father be one of those wishes?"

Theo was wondering the same thing.

"I do not speak of it," Reverend Thorne snapped. "I do not like to do anything that is connected with them. I am ashamed of my daughters and their choices, but there is nothing I can do."

"If that's true, why did you take us in, then?" Theo asked.

"Because you are family, and you were innocent. God deal with me ever so harshly should I fail to protect innocent blood."

"I need to know what you know about Annalora," Theo insisted. "If you want to protect other people, you need to tell me what you know. She's already aided a man who was trying to start a war between Rhone and Einish."

"What a foolish man."

"Foolish, maybe, but he still managed to endanger the lives of Philip's brother and his wife. And possibly their new baby," Theo said. He told them of what had happened in the castle at Crystal Lake, citing Juliette's fear and distress for her unborn child.

There was a small shuffling noise behind them as Theo finished his tale. He glanced over to see Bachas had come into the room.

"That's not all of it, either, by far," Bachas said. "She tricked my wife into a life debt. It was many years ago. Since then, she has used her to protect herself from any repercussions while she continues to oversee a majority of the Magdust trade."

Theo watched his grandfather's wrinkled face, usually as stoic as weathered leather, as it collapsed with despair. Theo and Thad each took an arm and guided him over to the chair where Rose had been sitting only moments before.

"Grandfather," Theo said, "you have to do something. All it takes for evil to prevail is that good people do nothing, remember?"

"I've already done nothing," the Reverend said. "It's too late. The kingdom is doomed. Annalora and Eleanora have already ruined it. They never should have made that Magdust tapestry for King Stefanos, even if he needed an heir."

Theo and Thad rounded on him.

"What are you talking about?" Thad asked. "You just told the Princess that she was a miracle baby."

The older man frowned. "I'm not saying anything else," he insisted.

"If you don't," Bachas spoke up, "I can make you change your mind."

"You can't use magic on me," the Reverend scoffed. "I'm a priest, remember?"

"I can still try," Bachas insisted. He stuck his tongue out at him. "And if nothing else, I feel no obligation to spare you any pain just using my fists."

"Ha! I'd love to see you try."

Theo stepped in between them. "There's no need for that. Just tell us the truth, Grandfather. Tell us what you know."

"I've kept the secrets of the kingdom for many years," the Reverend said.

"And they destroying us now," Theo told him. "Now, you must tell us the truth. Only that will allow us to make things right."

"You can't make things like this right."

"We can at least try, instead of sitting there and doing nothing!" Theo insisted. "Tell us."

Bachas took a menacing step forward, and the Reverend noticeably winced.

"Fine," he said. "Magdalina made a deal with Stefanos. She gave him Magdust in order to be able to conceive a child."

"Rose."

"The Princess, yes." The Reverend sighed. "The church was delighted, even though I knew it was magic. I did not say anything. Stefanos found out I knew, and threatened to remove me from the church."

"And you didn't resign or quit or transfer in protest?" Thad asked. "That's terrible."

"I wanted protection from your mother and aunt," the Reverend reminded him. "I wasn't about to leave the most connected sacred plot of land in the whole nation if I could help it."

"Did you tell the church the prophecy?" Theo asked. "The one you just told Rose about?"

"No," Reverend Thorne scoffed. "I'm not stupid. The King would have seen that as a desperate ploy for me to stay on his good side. The former head priest was the one who received it."

"So Rose is really a miracle?" Theo asked.

"Does it matter?" Reverend Thorne sniffed.

"It matters if you lied."

"Hardly."

"You say that, but it's your fault that Annalora is still on the loose, making tapestries full of Magdust."

"That's enough, Theo," Thad interrupted. "We have to get the facts first. Then judgment."

Theo scowled at him, but relented as Thad asked the Reverend about their mother's role.

"There's a problem with Magdust when you ingest too much of it. You can easily go insane. Magdalina poisoned the King with too much Magdust. He was slipping into madness. There was only one thing I could do, and … "

"So Mother and Annalora made a tapestry for him," Thad finished. "I see it now. You were the one who contacted them."

"Not directly," the Reverend said. "But Magdalina was determined to have the throne. She wanted Stefanos out of the way, no doubt, so she would be able to rule while the Princess was still a baby."

"And once Rose married Everon," Theo said, "everything she would finally have everything she wanted. She would have a kingdom of her own and a future for her son."

"That's about it," the Reverend said. "But when your mother and Annalora stepped in, and the King did not die, Magdalina was infuriated. She cursed Rose not only because he reneged on his promise that Rose would marry her son, but because he knew Magdalina had tried to kill him."

"If our mother saved the King's life," Thad asked, "why do you still avoid contact with Annalora?"

"Your aunt was very reluctant to help. She was upset and angry when Eleanora revealed what she was going to do with the tapestry. Annalora vowed never to work with her again, and she made certain threats at the time."

"So when our parents died," Theo said, "Annalora didn't know what had happened to them?"

"I doubt anyone knows for sure," the Reverend told him. "All I knew was what your uncle told me. There is a chance she knows something, but I couldn't tell you for certain."

There was a long moment of silence, and then Theo spoke up.

"I'll go and get her," Theo said. "Once we stop her, the Magdust trade will be down one supplier, and she can be brought to Rhone's capital for justice. And maybe her testimony will remind people that we need to band together to fight the Magdust trade once and for all."

"It's still too late. I failed her," Reverend Thorne whispered, his voice catching in his throat. It seemed that he had forgotten how to cry, to weep, to mourn.

Theo felt his sadness, so strained and unable to be released, as it weighed down on his weak shoulders. "It is tragic what happened to our family," he agreed.

"So many lives lost, so many people buying into empty promises, so many others caught up in the collateral damage," Thad muttered. "It's just awful."

Reverend Thorne sank deeper into the cushions. "It has been too many years. I can't just go and see her, or summon her."

"You're not able to travel well, anyway, Grandfather," Thad said. He turned to Theo. "He had trouble on the way here. We would have been here earlier if he had been able to handle the terrain better."

"I'm almost eighty-three," the man reminded him. "There's nothing wrong with me."

"There's nothing wrong with admitting that traveling across Rhone to meet with a formidable Magdust dealer might not be in your best interest," Thad pointed out.

"I already said I would go and get her," Theo said.

Theo did not like the idea of getting Annalora. He was certain Rose would be unwilling to go and bring Annalora to justice. Facing Magdalina and Everon had been their goal since he had set off with Rose over five years ago, and the thought of leaving her crushed him.

But as he watched his grandfather's face, Theo knew he had to do something. His grandfather, while he obviously did not like the idea of Thad and Theo running around in his church, had taken them in and raised them as much as he could. He had given them a home, and Thad a future. Theo knew he would never have met Rose without his grandfather taking him in.

Before Theo could ask for more details about Annalora again, Bachas snorted behind him. "I'd rather just kill her," he said.

"Bachas, please," Theo said. "This is a member of my family we're talking about."

"And she has my wife as her slave," Bachas reminded him. "I'm allowed my say, or do pixies not have the same rights as humans?"

"You can have your say," Theo told him. "But it is more a question of manners, than rights, and kindness over legalities."

The small pixie rolled his large eyes, almost eliciting a smile from Theo, before Bachas crossed his arms and stuck his nose up in the air.

"This is my fault," Reverend Thorne said. "I have been running away from all this trouble since the day Annalora and

Eleanora decided to follow their mother into the weaving business."

"It was still their choice," Theo said. "You don't get all the blame or all the glory when it comes to your child's choices."

"Let's hear you say that, and have a child who turns out as mine did," his grandfather scoffed. "Theo, the church is protected by magic. Why do you think I turned to the priesthood after my wife died? I knew all her troublesome activities would catch up to me one day."

"You know you should not use the church as a refuge for your own sin," Thad chided him lightly.

"It doesn't matter now. Annalora is my only child still left alive, and she is causing nothing but destruction for everyone who crosses her path."

Theo watched as Thad comforted their grandfather. A moment later, Bachas came up beside him, tugging on his pantleg. "What is it, Bachas?"

"I will go with you," he said. "I'll get everything ready while you talk to your princess."

"What makes you think I'm going to go now?" Theo asked.

"My seeing crystal," Bachas told him, holding up the small marble. "Why do you think I came here tonight? What business does a pixie have with a pair of priests otherwise? Besides, you know you are the most qualified and able to go. And you will. I have seen your heart, Sir Theo, and I know you always step up to help family."

Theo stilled. "What about Rose?"

"What about her?" Bachas frowned. "She has her own family to attend to, doesn't she?"

"But I'm her family."

"No, you're not," Bachas told him. "You're her partner, her protector, and her trusted advisor—until she needs to keep her heart and secrets safe from you."

"That's not true," he said, balking at his words. But Theo had a harder time dismissing Bachas' claims than he would have liked to admit.

"You've thought of leaving her before," Bachas chided him.

"For revenge," Theo muttered. "But I know now that I … I just can't leave her. And you really need to stay out of my mind."

"Seeing crystal," Bachas reminded him, holding up the small marble once more.

"Stop using it on me, then." Theo shook his head. "You don't get to tell me what to do."

"Even though I know what you'll do," Bachas whispered, his voice just sly enough to make Theo grimace. "Go and talk to your princess. See if I'm not right in the end. I'll be waiting for you in the stables."

Theo did not like the look on Bachas' face as the pixie left. There was a grim certainty on his face that made Theo nervous.

He struggled to shrug it off. He had work to do, he told himself. Thad was still arguing with their grandfather when Theo stepped forward.

"That's enough," he said. "If Annalora is as dangerous as we think, it is only right that I go and get her." He glanced down at the pixie beside him. "Bachas can come with me, to show me the way and to get his wife back."

The Reverend Father sniffed. "What makes you think you will convince her to come to Havilah and face me?" he asked.

ONCE UPON A PRINCESS

"I don't know," Theo admitted. "But you're too old, and you need to be here for Isra anyway."

"That's right." Thad straightened. "We have been sent here by the King to be his representatives. We need to work through her marriage contract and discuss her dowry with the Dowager Queen."

"I'm sure Utopa will be more than happy to discuss those details," Theo said. He turned to his brother. "Thad, why don't you come with me? I can give you back the manuscripts you lent us."

"I'll be more than happy to do just that," Thad said, brightening up at the mention of his scrolls. "I think it would be best if you find a way to rest for now, Reverend."

Their grandfather turned away from them and said nothing as they left.

"Do you think he was telling us the truth?" Theo asked Thad.

"Unfortunately, yes," Thad replied. "I have been going through the written records we house at the church. We have several thousand scrolls and books dedicated to testimonies the church has collected over the last several decades. But King Stefanos has very few, and he never makes much of an effort to come to mass or confession."

"If those are his secrets, I can see why."

"Yes, well, I suppose you've got a point."

They walked up to Theo's room, where he kept the manuscripts Thad had let them borrow. Thad cheerfully talked about other things, from the party to how nice it was to see everyone again.

Theo barely listened, as he thought about what Bachas said. It was only as Thad eagerly pawed through his papers that he said something that caught Theo's attention.

"What did you say?" Theo asked.

"I was wondering what Rose thought about what I told you before," Thad replied. "About true love's kiss. That has the power to break spells."

"I didn't tell her," Theo admitted.

"Why?" Thad grinned. "Too afraid she would look to Philip for deliverance?"

"No," Theo grunted, but he had to wonder if Thad was at least partially right.

"Oh, brother," Thad said. "You should really just tell her you love her. You said it yourself earlier: Truth will make things right."

"I don't know about that where Rose is concerned," Theo argued.

"Come on, Theo," Thad said. "Don't be such a hypocrite. You know it makes the rest of us look bad. And besides, sometimes you have to lead others by showing them the way."

"It was easier to tell that to the Reverend than it would be to tell her that." He did not want to tell Thad what Bachas had told him.

"Still, if true love's kiss would be enough to break her curse, she would want to know."

"Of all things, I know that's what she wants the most," Theo said. "Or at least, that's what she wants the most that she will admit to herself."

"Please," Thad said. "Just go and tell her."

"I should pack up and get ready to leave," Theo said, brushing his brother's concern aside. "After all, I have a lot more to think about right now, with everything we learned tonight about our family. Did you get your manuscripts?"

"Yes," Thad remarked. He gave Theo a hard look. "I'm going to get settled into my room," he said. "I'll talk with you again soon. I love you, brother."

"I love you, too." Theo gave him a smile as he left, glad that he did have family to support him, even when it was his own fear he found himself up against.

As soon as he was alone, he allowed himself to admit Thad was right.

If he wanted to know what was in Rose's heart, he would have to give her his first.

Long moments passed, as the music swelled from stories below. The night continued on, and the beauty of the night began to pass away into a quiet morning.

It was only then, after much thought and prayer, Theo made his way downstairs.

18

Not for the first time, Rose had trouble sleeping. It made no difference that on the night of her sister's engagement party, not too many other people were sleeping.

In fact, as she changed into her knight's clothes, and packed her things, she was comforted by the large gathering of people below. After a few hours of preparing to leave, Rose made her way out to the balcony of the ballroom once more, this time staying back and off to the side, watching all the dancers and cheers and eager faces as they slowly waned and began to tire.

Everyone is having such a good time, she thought.

Mary and Fiona were staying close to Philip and Isra, following them around even on the ballroom dance floor. Rose could see Ethan as he brought out his harp, strumming out a tune a few times here and there; even Sophia was there, in a fancy new dress Rose recognized as Mary's work, dancing with several elegantly dressed men. Rose smiled. *My kids are growing up, I guess.*

Which made the idea of leaving seem even harder.

After the ball, none of her friends would be eager to get back on the road to Rhone.

She had a lot of business to take care of, and there would be no fun such as this once she got back to her home. The King was under attack, either by another's hand or his own mind; the Queen Mother was in prison, and there was Uncle Hebert, whom she had trouble remembering if she ever even met, who was bringing an army to her mother's defense. And then there was the kingdom itself. How was she going to convince them that she was able to take care of them? That they could trust her, and that their nation would be safe?

"I don't even know the answer to that," Rose muttered to herself.

She sighed and turned away, and headed outside.

Back under the waning moonlight, she felt the tranquility of the moment before Lannister had come barreling into the gardens, before she had been called to meet with Reverend Thorne and Thad.

Everything seemed more potent, she thought, looking up at the early morning skies as they waited for the sun to rise. The earth seemed to breathe more easily. The flowers gave off their scent more freely. The air seemed more crisp.

"Rose."

Rose nearly jumped at the sound of Theo calling her name. Even his voice seemed more full of magic this morning, she thought as she turned to face him.

"Theo," she said. "What are you doing out here?"

"Probably the same as you," he replied. "I know you want to leave soon."

"I'm ready to go," Rose admitted. "I just don't know how to break the news to the others. I'm not even sure if I should make them go. Isra and Philip seem so happy here."

He nodded. "We have been moving around a lot in the last several months. I'm sure Philip is glad to be home, for sure. He hasn't traveled around as much as the rest of us."

"And I can't imagine Sophia and Ethan really want to go back to their home," Rose added.

Theo nodded. "What about you? Will you be happy to be back in Rhone?"

Rose bristled. "I doubt it. According to what your brother and the Reverend said, there are plenty of complications back home to keep me busy."

"I know how you feel." He came up next to her and held out his hand. "Why don't you walk with me for a while?"

"I don't need your arm," Rose told him.

"Come on, Rose," Theo said. "It's not that unusual. It's not like I'm asking you for your foot."

Rose smiled, even though she felt a rush of nerves. "Alright," she said, taking his hand.

She let him lead her down into the gardens. The music still played in the background, but the sounds of another world slipped away more and more with each step.

"This place seems magical," Rose said as they passed by several rose bushes. "Looking around, you could almost believe anything is possible. I feel like I could take on Magdalina herself in places like this."

Theo nodded. "I feel the same as you, but I'm curious as to how you would plan such a victory."

Rose had almost relaxed. She was glad they could talk about the upcoming battle, but she hated that he was going to ask her uncomfortable questions.

"After all," Theo said, "there's a chance the dragon's blood won't work."

"It's not like there is anything else that could," Rose replied, her tone hard.

She felt his hand tighten around hers. "Thad mentioned that there is something else that might work," he told her.

Rose stopped in her tracks. "What?"

"There's something else that might break Magdalina's spell," he said.

"If you're talking about marrying Everon—"

187

"No, I'm not," Theo told her. "Never that."

"What is it then?" she asked, genuinely curious now.

"True love's kiss."

Rose would have let herself laugh, if it wasn't for the look on his face. It was too serious now, and she could not stop her body from giving an involuntary shudder. "I don't believe it," she whispered. "It's too easy, and too hard, to just believe."

"You said this place felt full of possibilities. What about falling in love?" Theo asked, his voice quiet. "Why not?"

"Are we ever really free to fall in love?" Rose asked. "Because it seems to me that it just happens, and then there's very little to be done about it."

"There's still a choice," Theo said. He came up beside her, and she realized he was standing too close to her. Rose could feel the heat of his body. She could smell the sweetness of his breath. Hear the beating of his heart.

Rose knew she could have moved, but she did not. She stayed where she was, allowing him to be this close to her.

"How do you know?" she whispered.

"Falling in love and taking a leap of faith aren't so different, Rose." He reached out and took her other hand.

She felt her response immediately, and she knew he did, too. The shape of his hands, the feeling of his palms, the quiet trembling—she memorized all of it, taking in the strength and softness he radiated. She felt the bite in the wind as she inhaled sharply.

There was no one around this time. There was no Philip to come bursting through the door, no Mary to poke her head in, no Sophia and Ethan to interrupt them.

There was no one who would prevent her from making a choice; there was no one to stop her from making the choice she wanted to make.

Her eyes lifted to meet his. His emerald eyes, shadowed by the morning light and the misty fog, captivated her.

Rose knew in that second she was lost. She felt her body sway into his in silent surrender. Her eyes closed as he leaned down. For the briefest second, just before his lips touched hers, Rose went very still. And then she pressed up on her toes, aching for him. She felt the foreign press of his mouth against hers melt into a familiar caress. His lips fumbled against hers, just as she'd known they would; his scent consumed her, just as she'd known it always had. The taste of him scorched through her, just as she'd known it would.

Suddenly, she was kissing him as ardently as she'd known she'd always wanted to.

Rose pulled her hands free, wrapping her arms around his neck, her fingers digging into his back. She felt the desperation fueling them, as they struggled to move closer to each other, and matched his passion with her own.

"Rose," he breathed, pulling away from her only long enough to take another breath.

There was nothing she could do to protect herself.

He pulled away from her again, as his hands tangled up in her hair, his body pressed against hers. "I love you," he told her. "You know that, don't you? I'm in love with you."

All at once, the mood shattered. Fear flooded through her, and she quickly pushed him away.

Nothing had happened, Rose realized. There was no spell that had broken as she kissed Theo, save for the one where she could believe true love's kiss could work. "No," she said, shaking her head. "No, we can't do this."

ONCE UPON A PRINCESS

"Why not?" Theo asked.

"Magdalina's curse … nothing happened. I'm still the same as I was before we kissed. Her curse is still there." She tried not to slump over. "You don't have to pretend."

"I'm not pretending," Theo insisted, and before she could stop him, he was kissing her again.

Rose was unable to resist him, and the gentle urgency of his mouth. She trusted him. She knew he was telling her the truth.

He *was* in love with her, and she was in love with him.

Was this how it felt for Isra and Philip? Rose briefly wondered, as her pulse raced. If it was, Rose decided, she could see why Philip seemed so certain, and Isra was so determined. Theo's kiss overwhelmed her.

But just as she reveled in feeling his love for her, she knew the agonizing pain she would cause him. He loved her, and she was only going to end up hurting him.

As desperate as she was for him, she knew she had to save him.

"Theo," she murmured, allowing herself one last lingering taste of him.

"What?" His voice was breathless, and Rose suddenly felt like crying.

"I can't do this." She squared her shoulders and bravely tried to meet his gaze. "I don't love you."

"Don't you?"

"No," Rose whispered, unable to stop her voice from shaking. "And you don't really love me. I mean, we're friends. We've always been friends. You came with me because it was convenient, so you could find a way to get your own revenge—"

ONCE UPON A PRINCESS

"I have always followed you. And not because it was con-venient," he said. "I followed you because I wanted—"

"Because you wanted to."

"No, because I wanted you!"

Rose quickly stepped away from him. She did not want to hurt Theo—her strong, caring, compassionate, and loving Theo—all because he was in love with her.

"I know you, Rose," he said, taking her hand. He put her palm on his cheek. "I know you. I know you're lying."

"No, I'm not," she insisted, but her voice cracked.

"You wouldn't kiss me like that if it meant nothing."

Rose blushed furiously.

"You think you're protecting me," Theo told her. "But I know you're just trying to protect yourself." He let her hand go.

Rose felt her trepidation transform into anger. "Why shouldn't I?" she asked. "Why shouldn't I protect myself? If I don't want to love you, that's my choice."

"Is it?"

"Yes!" Rose shouted. She forced herself to meet his eyes with her own. "I don't want to love you."

He stared at her for a long moment, and Rose hoped he would not see how hard she was trying not to squirm under his imposing gaze. Her eyes slipped down to his mouth once more, and she stepped back even further from him.

"Please," she said. "Please, just leave me. I don't want you."

Of all the times she had fought with Theo over the years, she had never seen him take a blow like that. As she dis-missed him, he had a stricken expression on his face, a mix of disbelief and despair. Rose wondered if he would be in less pain if she had run her sword through his heart.

Finally, he gave her a slight nod. "If you won't let me love you, there is nothing more I can do here," he said. It was his turn to step away from her. "I have some family business to attend to in Rhone."

"You're leaving?" Rose asked incredulously.

"You want your space," Theo told her. "You'll have it. Please convey my regrets to the others."

"You're really leaving me?" Rose asked. "What about what you said earlier? About how you've always been a part of my life?"

"You also told me I need to protect myself from you," he said. "You've made your choice. I'm allowed to make mine, aren't I?"

Rose had to stop herself from wincing at his words.

He paused. "If you don't want me to go, all you have to do is tell me. You know I will do as you wish."

There was no way he was going to make her take full responsibility for this, she thought. Rose wondered if he was trying to make her admit it, to take back everything she had just gone through, in order to keep him by her side. Was it an ultimatum of sorts? Rose wondered.

She shook her head. "No," she said. "You're right. You should leave. Family matters, and I have my own family to deal with once we get to Rhone."

Theo looked crestfallen, but he nodded. "Alright, then. Goodbye … Rosary."

Rose watched as he turned away from her, surprised to feel a sharp pain inside her own heart, not relief. Rose curled her fingers into her palms, digging her nails deep into her skin, doing all she could to stop herself from calling him back.

As he disappeared back toward the castle, the tears finally slipped down her cheeks. She touched the rosary beads at her wrist, feeling the burning shame of her guilt.

19

Theo brushed against the rough wetness of his cheeks, let-ting their stinging saltiness sink into him as he entered the stables.

Bachas stepped out to meet him. "I told you we would be leaving," he said.

"I don't want to hear it," Theo said. "Please stop using your seeing crystal to see the future."

"I will tell you a secret," Bachas said. "I can see the future, but the future can still change. Everything I see is dependent on choices and circumstances."

"So you knew Rose would tell me to leave?" Theo asked.

"It was either that or give up the battle she has been fighting with her own heart for many years," Bachas replied. "And you know the Princess well enough to know she would never willingly give up a fight."

Theo nodded. "Well, let's head out then. Rhone is a good distance away from O'Lin by horse."

"Your brother is coming," Bachas said.

"Why?" Theo asked.

"I told him we were going to leave in the morning when he came to pester me with questions about pixie magic and their history."

Despite his sorrow, Theo smiled. "That's my brother for you," he said.

"Annoying."

"Sometimes." Theo shrugged. "But for the right reasons."

"If there are right reasons to be annoying."

"I'll remind you of that as we ride," Theo said. "I'm sure you'll have more of an argument for being annoying by the time you spend a whole day riding hard."

Bachas smirked playfully at him. "We'll see, Sir Knight," he said.

"I'm not a real knight. Not yet."

"Sure you are," Bachas said. "You've always wanted to follow in Benedict's footsteps, haven't you? Well, now that your lady has rejected you, your training is complete."

Theo's heart ached, and he struggled not to let Bachas see his pain. "I guess I wanted his success, but never his pain," he muttered.

"Theo?" Thad's voice called out from the far end of the stables.

"Over here," Theo replied, waving from his horse's stall. "We're about to head out, I guess."

"I'm glad I caught you," Thad said. "I'm so sorry we haven't had much time to catch up."

"We will have plenty of time," Theo promised, "as soon as I get back from Annalora's."

"Theo?"

"What?"

"You told her, didn't you?"

Theo cringed. "I don't want to talk about it," he said.

"But you did tell her?"

"For all the good it did," Theo replied. He sighed. "She wanted me to leave, so I am leaving."

"I will let her know why," Thad promised.

"If she cares at all," Theo grumbled.

"You know she does."

"She might, but she doesn't let herself do anything about it. Other than ignore it."

Thad shook his head. "I'm sorry," he said.

"It's fine. But Bachas and I are heading out." Theo turned to see the pixie climb up behind the horse's saddle, already working on a way to secure himself so he could rest easy on the way to Rhone.

"The Grand Father and I will be back in Rhone within a few weeks," Thad said to Theo. "Once we settle everything for Princess Isra, we will return."

Theo nodded. "I'll likely need some time to ride. Annalora's last location was near Aragon."

"Send me a message when you get the chance."

"I will." Theo clasped his brother's arm in his firmly, before he climbed up onto his horse, carefully avoiding Bachas as he swung his leg over. "Please take care of Rose for me."

"If she will let me," Thad replied. "Other than that, I'll do the best I can."

With that, Theo urged his horse forward, and he set off for Rhone. The moonlight has passed into sunrise, and the misty morning fog was already clearing itself from his path. The music of the ballroom had gone quiet, and the dew on the flowers was already starting to evaporate.

Behind him, Bachas sighed contentedly, relaxing as he settled behind Theo's saddle.

Theo tried not to think of all his friends as he left. He knew that he had to take care of his family, and he knew that Rose wanted the break between them. His heart was already in pain, and he needed to focus on the road as he headed toward Rhone.

As he passed through the last of the castle grounds, Theo reined in his horse, slowing down. He thought he could hear the music rising up from behind him again.

But once he could hear it, he knew what it was.

Who alone can be worthy of great love?
Our worlds are full of fools with dreams
Of tender kisses, melting looks, of
Magic underneath the moonbeams.

Queen Lucia sought to love a special one
Sir Benedict, his heart became the prize;
He who was worthy of her love alone
She saw as worthy in her own eyes.

He embraced her love and held her close
He fought for her hand and heart—
Only when he won did she choose
A life where they would never part.

Rose was singing to him.

"Goodbye, Rosary," he whispered once more, before he pushed his horse back into a trot. Theo knew he would be haunted by every moment over the past years that he was close to Rose; he already felt his heart breaking all over again, and it was more painful to know he would let it break forever if it meant he could kiss her again, if he could have her respond to him once more.

Theo knew he was free from her presence, but there was nowhere he could go where he would be free of her.

Of course, he thought to himself, that wouldn't mean he wasn't going to try.

"Hold on, Bachas," he called back, as he urged his horse into a full gallop. "It might get bumpy back there."

Bachas groaned as they sped up, heading out on a new adventure.

C. S. Johnson is the author of several young adult sci-fi and fantasy novels, including *The Starlight Chronicles* series, the *Once Upon a Princess* saga, and the *Divine Space Pirates* trilogy. She currently lives in Atlanta with her family.

ONCE UPON A PRINCESS

AUTHOR'S NOTE AND ACKNOWLEDGEMENTS

Dear Reader,

Over the many years I've had the privilege of traveling, I've noticed that the hardest part always seems to come in the middle of it—that part where you are not quite home, but the terrain begins to bend in that familiar way. It is frustrating, since you are so glad to be so close, but wearying, to know you are not quite there yet. I think this is what I most tried to capture in this book. Despite the progress, despite the encouragement, the human heart is always somewhat restless until it is secure in the knowledge that it has arrived to where it needs to be.

In the last book, I focused on the quest Rose faced, as she journeyed across the world. For this one, I wanted a more introspective journey, one that would force her to confront her own heart. Julius Caesar's famous assertion, courtesy of Shakespeare, that the courageous die only once is admirable, but when it comes to living, I am certain that introspective people (people who tend to be writers, unsurprisingly) live several, possibly innumerable, lives. The physical journey is often just as important as the inner journey, but life becomes even more than we thought it was, as we reflect on the different parts of what makes us who we are. Rose's journey here, to not only recognizing what is in her heart, but also making her choice to act on it, reveals the tension between idealism and realism, hope and hopelessness, and the fear of the choice and the choice itself.

It's all of life's little complications and all of the possible repercussions that make me excited to see what happens next.

As always, I am so grateful you took the time to read my work, and I hope you have enjoyed it. Please leave a review of it somewhere on the vast sea of the Internet, so I can see what you think—good or bad, I'm always interested to see what others think of my work. It's hard to see your work objectively as an author.

It shouldn't be a long wait until I finish the conclusion of this saga, *Beauty's Gift (Once Upon a Princess,* Part IV*)*. I'm looking forward to seeing you again soon!

Until We Meet Again,

C. S. Johnson

WORKS BY OTHER DIRE WOLF BOOKS AUTHORS

Wolf Code: A Sheltering Wilderness
Chandler Brett

A college student, Don, finds his dream career is at odds with the ideals his new-found love interest holds, even as his choices affect the survival chances for a pack of wolves. Check for more information at www.direwolfbooks.com.

The Adventures of Shamis and Larry
Jeff Sartini

An off-beat fairy tale adventure ensues as Shamis and Larry head off with a magical mule and a one-headed monkey. Check for more information at www.direwolfbooks.com.

ONCE UPON A PRINCESS

SAMPLE READING

Chapter 1 *from*

BEAUTY'S GIFT

PART IV OF THE *ONCE UPON A PRINCESS* SAGA

✳ ✳ ✳ ✳

C. S. Johnson

Courtesy of

www.direwolfbooks.com

1

It was an unescapable observation that, after years traveling across the world, seeing distant lands, meeting new people, fighting battles, and forging peace between fighters, Rose, the Princess of Rhone, found the day to day business of the king's council room seemed unforgivably dull by comparison.

Especially when her father used it as an excuse to herald his "brilliant" discoveries and decisions over the course of his reign, she thought, irritated as King Stefanos, as he continued droning on about some unrelated matter or another with one of his advisors.

Inside her father's council room, it seemed that it was business as usual, and that meant the king was intent on ignoring actual business.

She tried not to sigh in exasperation—again.

Even a princess has to learn how to deal with politics.

Moments, seemingly hours has passed as the knights of her father's council chatted, often getting off topic. Which would have been bad enough, but the topics were hardly relevant to the kingdom in the first place, Rose thought.

Finally, Rose had enough. She cleared her throat, cutting into the conversation. "Excuse me."

"What's wrong this time, Princess Aurora?" Stefanos asked, glaring down his nose at her.

Rose almost rolled her eyes. There was no need for him to look so repugnant. It was clear from his tone and his use of her proper first name he did not appreciate her interruption as he was describing the cuisine of the Orlo Empire.

"I was hoping we could move onto the next topic of the kingdom agenda, Your Majesty," Rose said, her own voice clipped. After several days of similar meetings, she could tell the King did not care she was getting impatient with him.

"We'll get there in a few moments. If you are feeling tired, you may be excused," Stefanos told her, chiding her as if she was a child. "I know this cannot be easy for an active young lady such as yourself."

Rose gave him a bitter smile. "I'm perfectly capable of sitting through a meeting, Majesty, but our subjects are more concerned with our decisions for the future, not stories of the past."

Stefanos' face reddened. He caught several looks around the table and suddenly laughed. "My daughter certainly has a bleeding heart for the people," he said. "No doubt they are much relieved to have her back in Rhone after all the years she has been abroad. Let us hope she will be able to learn how things are done here quickly, so we might truly be a force for good."

There were many nods and small voices of agreement around the table, before Stefanos once more turned the conversation back to himself.

Indignation simmered inside of her, but Rose held still. Since she had returned to Rhone several days prior, Rose had learned quickly that there was no stickier and messier battlefield to navigate than politics.

She breathed out a silent sigh as the King and his knights continued to laugh and joke as they half-discussed border security policies and taxation.

She was the heir to the kingdom's throne, and she had a right to be there as much as the King or any other of his knights—not that all of them would agree with that. As Rose looked around the table for support, she was not surprised to find many knights who avoided her gaze; of the ones who did look her way, most of them were glaring at her, suspicious. It did not help that several of the knights were older than her father, and years had passed since many of them had been sent out on assignment or they had fought in battles. Rose had her own ideas of who would be demoted the moment she took over the kingdom.

If I ever take over the kingdom.

As King Stefanos started telling another one of his stories, arguing for this or that, and the room resumed its informal, unserious atmosphere, Rose groaned.

If I ever get through this meeting.

Rose felt her eyes slip to the wall behind the King, wishing there was a window in the room. The room would have felt less like a prison.

A small amount of color in the council room would have brightened up the room considerably. After several days' worth of meetings where their subjects' concerns were either dismissed or endlessly debated, it would have been nice to have a reminder that they were responsible to their nation and its people.

Rose sighed as she thought about her trip home. It had taken her several days to ride through the countryside, going from one small village to the next, before crossing forests and open plains. Rhone was a smaller country, surrounded by others with a few port cities, where traders hustled and sellers would bring their goods out to market every day. Rose had seen it on her own grand tour, and she knew that her nation was as indebted to the sea as it was to the forest.

Thinking of the trip back to Rhone, one she had made with only the company of Mary, her fairy and friend, only made her think of the morning sky of Einish, and why she had been so desperate to get away.

She could see the sky as it glittered with early morning stars, the night of Isra's engagement ball. That was the night she had discovered her father's secrets, the night she had learned of her uncle's heavy-handedness, the night she had allowed herself to revel in a lover's kiss.

Theo's kiss. Rose could not resist reliving that moment, when his lips pressed against hers, and her heart ached with sudden pleasure.

At that thought, Rose quickly jolted out of her reverie. She gripped her hands together tightly, letting her fingernails dig into her knuckles. Pain wrecked through her, vivid and devastating, compounded by the weeks of carrying around her hidden longing and silent suffering.

That was the night she had last seen him. The early morning dawn had come just as she watched him vanish out of Einish's palace, and out of her life as well.

No.

Her hand slowly covered her heart, as if to steady its sudden, erratic beating. She almost cursed at herself. Several weeks had passed since she had seen him, and she still felt the same tumultuous rush of shame and regret. It was too much to bear, the thought that she would never see him again.

No, Rose thought. *I know him. He will come back.*

He had been her best friend for years. He had family matters to attend to, and then he would come back to Havilah.

But would he really come back? The voice at the back of her mind whispered. *You sent him away. You let him leave. You hurt him.*

Her head suddenly ached as much as her heart. Rose pretended to brush her hair out of her face as the prickly feeling behind her nose warned of unshed tears.

ONCE UPON A PRINCESS

Her attempts to feel better were always half-hearted and nearly useless, but Rose just could not make herself stop. She tried to console herself with the knowledge that he had family issues of his own to take care of, as he was going to find his aunt.

Surely, Rose told herself, she could understand that. She had her own family problems.

"That reminds me," she said, raising her voice as she glanced back up at the King. "Have you worked out any resolution with Uncle Hebert?"

At her words, the room finally went silent.

The king crossed his arms. "What are you talking about, Aurora?"

"I asked what you and others have decided to do about Uncle Hebert," Rose repeated. "He has been here for a little over a month now, hasn't he? What are you going to do about him?"

"Why do anything about him?" One of the other councilors asked. "He has not done anything wrong."

"You mean other than bringing in his own troops to patrol castle?" Rose crossed her arms over her chest. "Not to mention he has blocked off a number of visitors to the Queen since my return?"

Stefanos dismissed that matter with a wave of his hand. "Hebert is my brother," he said in even tones. "There is no cause for concern."

Before Rose could say anything else, Stefanos turned back to his friends. "Councilors," he said, "I'd like to adjourn our meeting for now. It's been a long day, and we have done much for the betterment of our people. You're dismissed. All of you may leave—except for you, Princess Aurora. Stay where you are."

Rose was surprised the king was going to hold her back. He had ignored her throughout the last several meetings, unless it was to chastise her or challenge her. But she knew Hebert was an important issue, despite what the king might have told his advisors.

She was almost concerned when the doors shut, the rest of the council members on the other side, and she found herself face to face with the King.

It was almost like last time, Rose thought, suddenly infuriated. Before she had left Rhone for the Serpent's Garden, she had talked with the King about her abdication, and he had not been happy with her decision to continue fighting for her freedom.

She was not surprised to see he looked even more upset with her this time.

"You need to stop this, Aurora," he said. "You can't keep coming to these meetings and expecting my men to support you when all you want to do is tear down my legacy."

"What legacy?" Rose huffed. "*I* am your legacy."

"I've done other things."

"Most of them more than thirty years ago."

"I am your father, and I am still your king. You need to show respect."

"I have," Rose insisted. "I've allowed you to sit here and waste time while we have real problems to deal with. There's our new treaty with Einish to finalize—"

"Isra's engagement *is* finalized."

"No, not that one. There's the new one, where we're pledging to help stop the Magdust trade from crossing our borders," Rose said. "We need to solidify our relationship with them if we're going to take on the traders."

"Isra's engagement—"

"Is finalized, I know," Rose interrupted. "But we still have plenty of time before she actually gets married. She's not even seventeen yet."

"You could have gotten married at sixteen, or even younger," Stefanos said. "Isra does not need to wait so long for that."

"She's still a child."

"A child of the crown, and therefore she must make certain sacrifices. It shames me that she knows this, and you don't, Aurora."

Privately, Rose knew that Isra had much more of a reason to be eager for marriage. Her younger sister had fallen in love with her betrothed, and Rose was even glad she would soon be able to count him as a brother. He was a good man, with a good family, and an even better friend.

"I know that just fine," Rose insisted. "But you know I am determined to make my own choices in the matter. After all, it wasn't my choice to be cursed by Magdalina, was it? It was hers, after you went to her to get some Magdust."

Stefanos' face instantly purpled with flustered rage. "You wouldn't be here if I didn't," he pointed out.

"But I *am* here," Rose argued. "There's no point in arguing out possibilities, Majesty. Not that you seem to be willing to discuss other, real problems we face. Including Uncle Hebert's presence here in Rhone."

"You need to stop talking about him," Stefanos hissed. "Aurora, these are my councilors. I'm not blind to the reality that they serve me at their leisure more than my command. Their armies and the people on their lands help protect us."

"I know that."

"But what you're forgetting is that Hebert used to live here, before I arranged his marriage to that Duchess of Aragon. He has his friends as much as I have mine on the council. They've remained loyal to him as well as to me. Don't ask me to make them choose, especially needlessly. They might choose him."

She was astounded to realize her father was afraid. He was afraid, she thought, and alone. Rose softened. She wanted to ask him if he thought the queen would choose Hebert, too.

"Maybe I can help you with Uncle Hebert," she said. "I can go and talk to him. And the queen, too."

Stefanos shook his head. "I don't want to make him upset," he said. "He was angry when I was the one who managed to bring the Rose Ruby back to Leea's father."

He began to pace the floor, wringing his hands nervously, as Rose reached over to her own wrist, feeling the rosary beads Theo had given her. She felt another wave of sadness.

"I can understand the fear of not being loved," Rose told her father quietly. "But I would not choose to sit around and do nothing."

He stopped at her words. "Aurora," he said. "That's all well and good, but sometimes you just don't know what to do as a leader."

I would at least stop all the meaningless chatter at our meetings, Rose thought, but she kept that to herself.

Stefanos shook his head. "My councilors are reluctant to face Hebert. And I am, too. You might not believe it, but he is doing me a favor by staying here."

"What?" Rose gaped at him. "What are you talking about?"

"He said he was here to protect Leea and oversee that she had a fair trial."

"Okay, well, the queen's trial is coming soon," Rose said. "Right?"

"Once we get through the rest of the kingdom's problems," Stefanos told her.

"You've delayed it plenty of months," Rose argued. "Can't we just go through with the trial, now that I'm home?"

"No, Aurora, that's not how that works."

"How that works is wasting time!"

"It is not wasting time if it is in accordance with the kingdom," Stefanos snapped back.

"I don't understand why you just don't change it," Rose said.

"I have my reasons, just like I have my secrets," he told her firmly.

What's that supposed to mean? Rose wondered. She had discovered some of his secrets, and she knew that they were more shocking than she would have liked. She hated to think that his reasons for his actions could somehow be worse.

"In the meantime, you're better off worrying about your own problems, Aurora. You've been here for the past several weeks, interfering with my work and trying to usurp my meetings."

"This is my kingdom, too."

"But it is under my rule right now, and you should respect that." Stefanos shook his head. "For now, just stay away from Hebert and his guards. And stay out of my council room, too. I have too much to do, and you're getting in the way of my work."

Rose felt insulted.

"Besides," Stefanos said, "your siblings are due to arrive from Einish with Prince Philippos any day now. You might as well see to the castle, especially since your mother is occupied otherwise."

It took more willpower than Rose would have liked to admit to grit her teeth together and say, "Yes, Your Majesty," before she stomped out of the room.

OTHER WORKS BY THE AUTHOR

The Starlight Chronicles, by C. S. Johnson

Everyone has a set of beliefs that sets them apart from others.

When a meteorite strikes the heart of Apollo City, sixteen-year-old Hamilton Dinger finds all of his beliefs—mainly in himself—unable to stand against the reality of his supernatural powers. Tensions increase as the meteorite unlocks the Seven Deadly Sinisters, and their leader, Orpheus, and they begin to attack the city's citizens. With Elysian, a changeling dragon, and Starry Knight, a beautiful but dangerous warrior, Hamilton must overcome his inner struggles, seal away the bad guys, and still finish his homework. Join Hamilton throughout this seven-book series as he becomes the superhero Wingdinger and sets out to save the day … and the world.

The Divine Space Pirates, by C. S. Johnson

If survival is all that matters, does truth still make a difference?

There is nothing Aerie St. Cloud wants more than her family unit's love—until she is accidentally captured by the fearsome space pirate, Captain Chainsword, and she is stuck on his pirated starship, the _Perdition_. Aerie soon realizes the difference that the truth does make, as she finds herself falling in love with the tragic space pirate captain. Can her love help bridge the gap between her worlds? Or will it just lead to more destruction?

MORE BOOKS ON THE WAY!

SIGN UP FOR THE MAILING LIST!

Get emails full of updates and insights, and possible prizes when you sign up for the mailing list! Sign up at https://www.csjohnson.me.